The Day of Their Wedding

WILLIAM DEAN HOWELLS

# The ay of Their Wedding

MASTERWORKS OF FICTION
(1895)

GREEN INTEGER
KØBENHAVN & LOS ANGELES
2006

GREEN INTEGER BOOKS
Edited by Per Bregne
København / Los Angeles

Distributed in the United States
by Consortium Book Sales and Distribution
1045 Westgate Drive, Suite 90,
Saint Paul, Minnesota 55114-1065
Distributed in England and throughout Europe by
Turnaround Publisher Services
Unit 3, Olympia Trading Estate
Coburg Road, Wood Green, London N22 6TZ
44 (0)20 88293009

(323) 857-1115 / http://www.greeninteger.com

First Green Integer Edition 2006
Originally published as *The Day of Their Wedding*
(New York: Harper and Brothers, 1895)
Back cover copy ©2006 by Green Integer

Design & Typography: Trudy Fisher
Photograph of William Dean Howells

LIBRARY OF CONGRESS CATALOGING IN PUBLICATION DATA
William Dean Howells [1837-1920]
*The Day of Their Wedding*
Green Integer 145 / ISBN: 1-933382-71-6
I. Title II. Series

Green Integer books are published for Douglas Messerli
Printed in the United States on acid-free paper.

# The Day of Their Wedding

# I

WHEN the train slowed before drawing into the station at Fitchburg, Sister Althea took up her bag from the floor, and began to collect her paper parcels into her lap, as if she were going to leave the car. Then she sat gripping the bag to her side and staring out into the night, blotched everywhere with the city lights and the railway signals — red and green and orange. From time to time she looked round over her shoulder into the car, up and down the aisle, and again set her face towards the window, and held it so rigidly, to keep herself from turning any more, that it hurt her neck.

The car was a day-coach on a night train, and most of the few passengers were taking preparations for leaving it. An old gentleman in the seat across the aisle, whom she had asked more than once whether the train was sure to stop at Fitchburg, was already buttoned up in a light overcoat, which he had the effect of wearing in compliance with charges against exposing himself to the night air. He sat humming to himself while he held fast an umbrella and a bundle such as one married sister might send to another by their father; it was in several sections of wrapping-paper, and was tied with tape. He leaned over towards Sister Althea, and asked, benevolently, "Was you expecting to meet friends in Fitchburg?"

Sister Althea started and looked round. He repeated the question, and she gasped out, "Nay; I am not expecting friends to meet me." She had framed her reply with a certain mechanical exactness which he seemed to feel.

"Oh! ah! From the Family at Yardley, I presume?"

Sister Althea faltered a moment before she answered, "Yee."

She let her head droop forward a little, and with her Shaker bonnet slanting downward over her deeply hidden face she looked like a toucan, except for the gayety of color with which nature mocks that strange bird's grotesqueness. She was in Shaker drabs as to her prim gown, and her shawl crossed fichuwise upon her breast; her huge bonnet was covered with a dove-colored satin. To the eye that could not catch a glimpse of her face, or rightly measure her figure as she sat dejected for the moment following her speech, she must have looked little and old.

The friendly person in the seat opposite began humming to himself again. He stood up before the train halted, and he said to Sister Althea, as he turned to leave the car, "Well, I wish you good-evening."

"Good-evening," said Sister Althea, faintly; and now, when the train stopped at last, and the noises of the station began to make themselves heard outside, with the bray of a supper-gong above all, she jumped to her feet and started into the aisle as if she were going to leave the car too. She even made some steps towards the door; then she came back, and, after a moment's hesitation, she sat down again, and remained as motionless as before.

People came and took places, and arranged their wraps, and put their parcels into the racks, and settled themselves for their journey. Among the rest a woman came in, followed by a man with a child. When he had put the child in the seat beside her, he stood talking with her till she drove him away. She said she did not want him to get off after the cars began to move. He laughed and kissed her, and after he had got almost to the door he came back and kissed her again. Sister Althea trembled at each kiss. When the man lifted the little one and kissed it, and put it down again on the seat beside its mother, the tears came into her eyes.

"Well, give my love to all the folks!" he called back from the door.

"Yes, yes!" said the woman. "Do get off, quick!"

He laughed again, and in looking back from the door he struck against a young man who was coming in. "Oh, excuse *me!*" he said, and went out while the young man came forward. He looked from side to side keenly, and then, with a smile that flashed through Sister Althea's tears, he came swiftly down the aisle to where she sat, near the end of the car.

"Well, well!" he cried, and he stood a moment with his hands upon the seat-backs, looking down at her where she sat, helpless to move her bag and parcels from her side. "A'n't you going to let me set with you, Althea? A'n't you going to look round and let me see if it's really you? First, I didn't know but it was Eldress Susan."

"'Sh!" said Sister Althea, and she turned up towards him the deep tunnel of her bonnet, with her young face at the bottom of it, and clutched her parcels into her lap.

He swung her bag to the floor, and let himself sink easily into the seat, and stretched his arm along the top behind her. "Oh, I guess she won't hear us," said the young man. "Did you know me when I came into the car? I don't believe you did!" He laughed, and his eyes shone. They were gay blue eyes, and his hair, now that he took his soft hat off, had glints of gold in the dun tone that the close shingling of the barber gave it. His face was clean shaven and boyishly handsome. He was dressed in a new suit of diagonals which betrayed the clothing-store; but his figure was not vulgar, though his hands, thrusting out of the coat-sleeves without the shirt-cuffs that might have partly hidden them, were large and red, and rough with work. "I saw you through the window as I came along the platform outside, and I wanted to stop and watch you. But you had your head down, as if you wa'n't feeling any too bright, and I hurried right in. I thought you would be frightened if I didn't come in as soon as the cars stopped. But I was waiting here so long expecting the train that I forgot to get my bag checked till the last minute, and I had to run and do it after you got in. That's what kept me. Did you think I wa'n't going to be here, after all?" He let his arm drop from the seat-top, and he sought with his the little hand lying weak on the seat between them. It closed upon his fingers at their touch, and then tried to free itself, and then trembled and remained quiet. "Oh, I guess I did frighten you," he murmured, fondly.

"Hush! Yee," said Althea. "But I knew you would be sure to be here. I wasn't afraid, but I was — scared a little. I was anxious. When you came in I could see it was you, but you looked so strange." She cast a glance up and down the car.

"Don't you like it?" he asked, with a smile of innocent pride and a downward look at his clothes.

"Yee, yee," she said. "But, Lorenzo, do you think — do you think you had ought to — sit in the same seat with me — so close? Won't folks —"

Lorenzo laughed securely. "Think I ought to set across the aisle, same as in meeting? I guess folks won't mind us much." In fact, in the going and coming and settling in place no one seemed to notice them. "If they do, they'll think I'm just your brother or some relation. It's this old bonnet, if anything, that will make them look. I thought Friend Ella Shewall was going to lend you a hat."

"Yee, she was. But I didn't get to her house till it was almost time for the cars, and then we had to just race to the depot. I've got the hat here in this paper, and that's a sack in this bundle. I hadn't time to put it on, either. I was almost ready to drop when I reached Friend Ella's." He peered into the depths of the bonnet she turned towards him, and she added: "I ran nearly the whole way from Harshire to the Junction."

"Ran?"

"Yee. I couldn't get out of the house without some of the Family seeing me before dusk; and if they had I should have died. I was so *ashamed*, Lorenzo, and I felt so *mean*, I can't tell you! I kept close to the walls and in the woods all I could, and I had this bag —"

Lorenzo stooped forward and lifted the bag from the floor. "You carried that all the way from Harshire to the Junction?"

"Yee."

"Well!"

"I didn't feel it. It wasn't the *bag* that was so heavy. Oh, Lorenzo, do you think we're doing right?"

"I know we are! Why, Althea, it's what everybody does in the world-outside."

"In the world-outside, yee."

"Well, we're *in* the world-outside, ain't we?"

"Yee, I presume we are. We are going to be of the earthly order, Lorenzo; we are going to give up the angelic life! Have you thought enough of it, Lorenzo? Do you think you have? Because if you haven't —"

"Why, haven't we both thought of it till we couldn't think any more? What did Friend Ella Shewall say? Didn't she say that we ought to take our feelin' for each other as a sign from spirit-land that we were meant for each other from all eternity?"

"Yee; but she isn't living with her own husband; she's trying to get a divorce from him, and she used to be so fond of him."

"Well, then, the signs failed in her case —"

"Oh, don't laugh at it, Lorenzo! If they failed in ours, what should we have? Am I worth all you're risking for me in this world and the next? Think of it, Lorenzo! I can get out at the next stopping-place and go back to the Family; I know they'll let me; and you — Think of it! *Am* I worth it?" She spoke in a low, intense whisper.

"Am *I*?" retorted the young man, lightly.

"Oh yee! *You* are! I'd go through it all for you."

"Then I guess that settles it."

"Nay, nay; it doesn't! I'm wicked, and that's why I feel so. You don't know how bad I am. I *deceived!* It was all right for you, for you left the Family open and above-board, and you told the Trustees you were going, and you made them give back your property and everything; but I *stole* away like a thief in the night; and I made Friend Ella take part in my deceit; and, Lorenzo, I don't believe there's going to be any end to it. I've told two lies already, here in this very car — just before it stopped. There was a man asked me whether I expected to meet friends at Fitchburg, and I said nay; and he asked me if I wasn't from the Family at Yardley, and I said yee, I was, and —"

"He no business to asked you anything," said Lorenzo, hotly, "and I d'know as you can call it lyin', anyway. I a'n't friends in the sense he meant, and Yardley and Harshire, it's almost the same thing, and it don't matter which Family you come from, so you're out of it."

"Do you think so, Lorenzo?"

"Yee, I do. And now look here, Althea; you're nervous, and you can't see things in the true light, and so everything looks wrong to you. We're doing what we have a perfect right to do, and what everybody in the world-outside does, as I said before. If you had to steal away, as you call it, from the Family, whose fault was it? 'Twa'n't yours. You did it, if anything, to save their feelin's, didn't you?"

"Yee, I presume so."

"Don't you *know* you did? Now I want you to try and look at it in the light of the world-outside; for that's all the light we've got now, or that we're going to have."

A little troubled sigh exhaled from the depths of the bonnet, and Lorenzo threw himself back in despair. "Oh, well, if that's the way you're goin' to feel about it."

"Nay, nay, Lorenzo! I'm not going to. I shall be all right in a minute. I'm just nervous, that's all. I think just as you do about it. Wasn't I perfectly willing and glad to do it?"

"I guess you wa'n't half so willing nor half so glad as I was," said the young man, and now he drooped towards her again. "And, as you say, I had the easiest part of it, too, as far forth as getting away from the Family went. But, Althea," he added, with a touch of pride, "I haven't had a very easy time since I've been in the world-outside. 'Ta'n't but a few days, but it seems as if it was years, worrying about you all the while, and trying to sell my lot in Fitchburg, and look up something for me to do when we get back."

"Yee, we have got to think of that now, I suppose," said Althea. "In the Family it came without our thinking."

"Yee, too many things came there without our thinking," said Lorenzo, resentfully. "Not that I want to talk against the Family. I presume I feel just as you do about that. Our own fathers and mothers couldn't have been better to us. But if we was to have each other, we *had* to leave 'em. There wa'n't any two ways about it. And I guess I do like to think for myself, even of my bread and butter. And I guess I've arranged for all that. I'm going into the drug business with Friend Nason."

"That used to come and buy our herbs at Harshire?"

Lorenzo nodded. "It's just the place for me. He's goin' to put a new remedy on the market for lung difficulty — Pulmine, he calls it — and he wants me, because I know about herbs; it's going to be purely vegetable. He's bought my lot, too, and he's advanced me a hundred dollars on it." The young fellow leaned a little nearer and tapped his breast-pocket. "I've got it with me! And I've seen the nicest little set of rooms for us to go to house-keeping in when we get back. Friend Nason calls it a flat; and I guess when you see that kitchen, Althea! Friend Nason says it's just as well we're going to Saratoga, for we sha'n't have to get a license in York state; and if it had to be in Fitchburg, and we was to settle down there, right from the Family, it might make talk. But if we come back just like anybody else from the world-outside it'll all blow over before any-body notices. He wouldn't want it to get into the newspapers any more than we would or the Family would."

# II

THE train, which had started long before, advanced by smooth leaps through the dark, and the rhythmical clangor of the wheels upon the rails lost itself in Lorenzo's tones while he talked on and mapped out the future to Althea. Already, though he had been so few days in the world-outside, he knew many things unknown to her, and he looked at everything from a point of view that she could not yet imagine. He used words that she had never heard before, and he used familiar phrases in a new sense. He spoke low, and not to lose anything he said she had to turn her deep bonnet towards him, and peer up into his face with eyes so still and solemn in their fixity that at last he laughed out.

"What are you laughing at?" she half grieved.

"Oh, nothing. Your eyes down there in that old bonnet made me think of a rabbit that I got into a hole once, and it kept looking up at me. What is there to scare anybody, anyway, Althea?"

"Nothing. I'm not scared now."

"Well, I believe it's that bonnet, after all. Why don't you take the old thing off?"

"I don't know. They would look."

She glanced round the car at their fellow-passengers, and Lorenzo did so too. "Well, *let* them look!" he said, with a petulant impulse; and then, as if he had given way too far, he added, "They've all got their backs turned, anyway."

"So they have!" said Althea. "I took this seat at the end of the car on purpose, so they wouldn't notice me so much. I forgot about that."

Still she did not offer to remove her bonnet, and he repeated, "Why don't you take the old thing off?"

"Do you truly want me to?"

"Yee; I want to see how you'll look."

"Why, you know already how I look with my cap on."

"Got that on too?"

"Yee."

"Oh, what's the use of *yeeing* and *naying* it all the time, Althea? We've got to say yes and no after this."

"You said yee yourself half a minute ago."

"Did I?" asked Lorenzo; and after a moment's thought, he said, "Well, so I did," and he laughed at himself. "But it's all that old bonnet makes me do it. I say yes to other folks straight enough. Do take it off!"

"Well, I will, if you want I should so very much," said Althea, and she kept watching his face while she began to undo the bonnet strings.

"Want I should help you any?"

"Nay; I guess I can get along."

"There's that nay again!" said Lorenzo, desperately, and they both laughed. "Take off your cap, too. Wouldn't you just as lives?"

"Yee, if you say so."

"There it goes again!" And they laughed together, but very softly, so that the other passengers should not notice. The woman with the child was making up a bed on the seat in front of her for the little one; she looked over her shoulder a moment, but she did not seem to take them in with her vague glance. Althea stopped untying her bonnet-strings, and then went on. She lifted the drab tunnel from her head at last, and showed the wire-framed gauze cap, closely fitted to her head. "Now the cap," said the young man, and she untied that too, and took it off, and turned her face full upon him.

She looked like a pretty boy, with her dark hair cropped to her head all round, and her severe turn-down collar, which came so high up on her throat that her soft round chin almost touched it. She had dark eyes, very tender and truthful, a little straight nose, and a mouth that smiled unspeakable question at the young man with its red lips; delicate brows arched themselves above her dove-like eyes, and her forehead was a smooth and white wall to the edge of her hair. The ugly bonnet had served well to keep her complexion fair; its indoors pallor had now a faint flush in it.

Lorenzo caught his breath, and turned his face with a slight cough.

"What is the matter? Have you got a cold?" she asked.

"Nay. It seemed as if my heart skipped a beat. I guess it was the surprise."

"Do I surprise you very much, Lorenzo?" her pretty lips entreated, fondly. "Do I look so very funny? You made me do it!"

"Nay, nay! You look — beautiful, Althea. I

don't know as I ought to say it, Althea, but I didn't know how beautiful you was before." He stared at her so helplessly and awe-strickenly that she could not help laughing.

"You're fine-appearing, too, Lorenzo. I noticed it when you came into the car. I presume it's my hair that makes me look so funny. But it isn't half as short as yours," she said, with an arch glance at his hair as far as it showed itself under his hat. He took his hat off, and she pressed her hand against her mouth to keep from laughing too loud. "I guess we're a pair of them!"

He still sat embarrassed, looking at her, and studying every little motion of her head and face as she put her cap inside her bonnet, and made as if to tie the string of the bonnet over both. "But maybe," she said, "you want I should put them on again?"

"Nay," he began, and she mocked him with "*Nay!* There it is again!" But he would not laugh.

"Althea, I don't hardly feel as if I had any right to you. It's all well enough to talk, but I didn't know that till you looked — the way you do look; and if you say, I'll give up right now."

"And what shall *I* do if you give up now?" she

asked, with eyes full of laughter.

"That's true," he sighed.

"I didn't know how well you looked, either, till I saw you with that suit of clothes on."

"Do you like them?" he asked, with a proud glance at the sleeves of his coat and the legs of his trousers. "I had to pay twenty dollars for the suit. Friend Nason thought it was a good deal — he went with me — but he said he guessed I better have them if I was going off with you; I'd get more comfort out of them than what I would a cheaper suit."

"Yee," said Althea, thoughtfully. " If we're in the world-outside we have got to do the same as the rest." She drew a little away from him to add, with a touch of tender reproach, "But I began to feel foolish about *you*, Lorenzo, long before I saw you in that suit of clothes — as foolish as I *ever* could."

"And I felt foolish about you when I couldn't hardly see your face in the bottom of that bonnet, let alone know what a pretty head you had, or anything. It was something the way you walked — I d' know — and your — your waist, Althea —"

She turned away from him to take up the parcel on the other side. She put it in her lap, and asked, "Do you want I should show you the sack Friend Ella lent me?"

"Why, yee; of course!"

"She said it was quite the fashion." Althea undid it and held it up and whirled it about, so that the jet trimming would show, and she made him feel the texture of the silk. "Now, I'll try it on if you want I should." She flung it across his knees, and unpinned the Shaker shawl from over her breast, and let it fall from her shoulders. She stopped suddenly with a fiery flush.

"What is it?" asked Lorenzo. He looked in the direction of her eyes, and saw one of the men passengers coming straight down the car towards them; but the man went on to the water-cooler in the corner just beyond them, and after he had solemnly filled himself up from the tank there he lumbered back to his place again at the other end of the car. They looked at each other as people do who have had a narrow escape. Althea pulled the shawl up on her shoulders again. "I guess I'll wait till morning to put it on."

"Yee, just as well," said Lorenzo, and he could

not have seen the filmy shade of disappointment that passed over her face. "What are you going to do with that old thing?"

He touched her Shaker bonnet, and she glanced down at it. "Oh, keep it, I presume," she sighed — "keep it always. Any rate, I shall keep it till morning." She tied it up with the paper that had wrapped her sack.

Lorenzo rose from the seat and stood beside it. "Look here, Althea, I'm going back into the sleeping-car here to get a place for you, so you can rest comfortable. I don't want you should sit up here all night."

"What are you going to do?"

"Oh, I can set up well enough —"

"Then so can I, too! And I'm going to stay here with you."

"Now, Althea, you just let me have my own way about this. I took the place for you before the car reached Fitchburg, and it's paid for, and you might as well use it."

She would have protested further, but he had already left her, and she vainly appealed to him with her entreating eyes when he looked back at her over his shoulder.

While he was gone she unwrapped the hat that she had borrowed from Friend Ella Shewall, and put it on at the little mirror by the water-cooler. Then she dropped her Shaker shawl over her arm, and sat down again to wait.

When Lorenzo came back he started at sight of her. "Well, well!" he said.

"Do you like it?" she cooed back at him.

"Well, I should think so!"

He began to pick up her bundles, and she stood outside of the seat to give him a chance. "I thought I wouldn't like to have them see me in my Family shawl and my short hair," she explained.

"I guess they wouldn't noticed much," said Lorenzo. "There a'n't anybody up but the porter. Well, it's all ready." He stopped, and let some of the parcels fall back into the seat, and stood staring at her.

"What is it?"

"Nothing," he answered; and then he said, thickly, " I was just thinking how you would look in a dress that I saw a girl have on at Fitchburg to-day." She felt his eyes on her waist, but she did not mind; she laughed for pleasure; she liked to know he thought she had a pretty waist; he might just as well. He affected to turn it off with a practical remark: "That dress looks a little Shaker yet. Perhaps it won't when you've got the sack on over it. Anyway, we can get something ready-made at Saratoga. I don't believe you'll ever get anything that'll fit you much better," he gasped, in helpless adoration.

The girl's face fell a little. "Yee. Sister Miranda made it. She said she was afraid she took almost too much pride in it. I did hate to leave without saying good-bye to her!"

"Yee," said the young fellow, gravely.

The black porter from the sleeping-car came in briskly, and after a glance up and down their car to make sure of his passenger he came and took Althea's bags and parcels from Lorenzo's passive hands. "This way, lady," he said.

She looked at Lorenzo, and he nodded. "I guess he can show you."

"Good-night," she said, following the porter out.

"Well, good-night," answered Lorenzo. He sat down in the seat now empty of her form, and pulled his hat over his eyes.

# III

IT was bright day when she came back to him from the sleeping-car, but he had not yet awakened. She stood looking down at him and smiling, and presently he started awake and stared distractedly up at her before he could pull himself together and say, "Well, well! Did you sleep pretty well?"

"I *rested* pretty well," she answered. "How did you?"

Lorenzo laughed. "I guess I slept pretty well, but I don't believe I rested very much. But I've got the whole day to rest in now." Althea had Friend Ella Shewall's hat and sack both on, and she waited for him to realize the fact before she sat down. "Well, well," he said, in recognition, "that sack *is* nice."

"Well?" she urged, as if she felt a disappointment in his tone.

"Well, what do *you* think?"

"It don't seem to go exactly with the dress."

"Nay," said Lorenzo, with his laugh. "It makes

you look like the world-outside one-half, and the other half Shaker."

"Yee, it does," said Althea, forlornly; her chin trembled a little, and her eyes threatened tears. "I guess it's all we're ever going to be, too, Lorenzo: half Shaker and half world-outside," she added, bitterly. "I guess I better go back into the sleeping-car and put on my old shawl and bonnet again."

"No such a thing!" cried Lorenzo. "I guess we'll see about that when we get to Saratoga — we must be pretty near there now. Set right down here, and I'll go back for your things."

"Nay, the colored man said he would bring them." Althea sank into the seat and got out the handkerchief, broad as a napkin, which she had brought from the Family with her, and wiped the tears from her eyes. Then she bowed her face into it, and her little frame shook with the sobs she smothered.

"Well! well!" groaned Lorenzo, in an anguish of tenderness.

Althea suddenly took her handkerchief away and controlled her face. "There! I am ashamed, Lorenzo."

"Nay, don't you say that, Althea. You've got just as much right to cry as anybody, and I *want* you should cry."

"Nay, I've got through now," said Althea; and to prove it she smiled up into his face so radiantly that he laughed, and she laughed with him.

The porter with her bag and parcels perhaps thought he had arrived at a fortunate moment. He set the bag respectfully at her feet, and kept a smiling face on Lorenzo while he arranged the parcels almost decoratively on her lap. Then he lingered a moment; the smile died on his face, and he went mournfully away. They both felt the gloom in his manner, and were sensible of a vague reproach in it.

"What was it, Lorenzo?" she asked.

"Well, that was just what I was going to ask you, Althea," said Lorenzo. They wondered over the incident so sadly closed, and their minds were not wholly taken from it until they drew in sight of Saratoga and the train began to slow. They ran along the backs of some simple houses whose yards and gardens were shorn off by the track, and then the vast bulks of the hotels began to show among the foliage that everywhere masses itself over the town. "This must be it," said Lorenzo, and they looked at each other in a sudden fright. "No use being scared about it now," he added, as he resolutely gathered up Althea's belongings and stood aside to let her get out of the car. The conductor who took her elbow to help her down from it let Lorenzo shift for himself, and the embarrassment they felt was relieved for them both by his dropping some of the parcels, and their having to pick them up from under the feet of the crowd thronging into the station. She made him let her keep some of them now, and they passed through the station to the street beyond, where there was a clamor of carriage drivers, and a rank of stately hacks and barouches, and light, wood-colored surreys and phaetons. The drivers swarmed upon them, but as they stood silent and motionless under their burdens the drivers dropped off one by one, like dogs that have rushed out at a passer and have failed to make the expected impression upon him. At last they were free, and they walked from the station under the flank of a mighty hotel into a wide street, where they found it one hotel of many, with sweeping piazzas and narrow pillars springing into the air like the stems of tall young trees. The street was freshly watered, and smelled of the dampened dust; it was set with elms, and under their arches stood vehicles of the same sort and variety as those at the station. Some drove slowly up and down through the sun and shadow; but their drivers, after a glance at Lorenzo and Althea struggling along under their parcels, intelligently forbore to invite them to a morning drive.

"I guess we sha'n't want to go to any hotel just yet," said Lorenzo. "We can get breakfast at an eating-house, if we can find one."

"Yee," Althea timidly assented.

They had to walk up and down a long while before they found an eating-house. Lorenzo began to be afraid there was nothing but hotels in Saratoga. They trudged along, staring at all the signs, and the shopkeepers, sweeping the dust of their floors across the pavement to the gutters, had to stop for them to get slowly by or else sweep it against them. Althea knew that Lorenzo looked well, but she was smitten with a sense of her own inadequate appearance, and she tried to shrink as much out of sight as possible.

"Here's one at last," said Lorenzo, stopping at a doorway. "Go right in, Althea," he added to her at a certain faltering she showed. "It's all right. It's just like the one Friend Nason took me to in Fitchburg."

It seemed very splendid with its mirrors and marble-topped tables and bent-wood chairs, and it overcame Althea with the surprise and then the indifference it showed in the shining black waiter who came forward after a moment, as if their custom were not expected or much wanted at that hour in the morning. But Lorenzo was not afraid. He asked if they could have something to eat; and then the waiter said he guessed so, and he took their parcels and set them against the wall by the table he chose for them. Little groups of flies had knotted themselves into rosettes on the marble where it seemed to have been imperfectly cleansed; others paraded across it in black files. There were a great many flies in the long, narrow saloon, and the air within was faint and dull, as if it were the air of the evening before, and had been up all night there. A man was wiping a marble counter with a soda fountain at one end of it. At the rear of the room a boy was taking down the chairs which stood on the tables with their legs up.

Lorenzo asked Althea what she wanted for breakfast, and when she could not think he told the colored man he guessed they would have beefsteak and coffee and hot biscuit. The colored man said they had no hot biscuit yet, and he suggested hot cakes.

"Well, hot cakes, then," said Lorenzo; and he said to Althea that he guessed hot cakes would be full as well anyway.

Before he brought their breakfast the waiter spread a large napkin over the marble before them, and that forced the flies into a momentary exile. They rose into the air, but they did not go far; they remained circling round overhead and humming angrily till Lorenzo's order came, and then they settled down upon the table again, and brought with them apparently all the other flies they knew.

The steak was very juicy and tender, and when the cakes came from the place where an old negro stood frying them on a slab of soapstone with gas-jets underneath they were very good too. But the coffee was green in color when they had poured their small jugs of milk into it, and thick with grounds.

"Not much like our cocoa at the Family," said Lorenzo, for a joke.

Althea let fall a small "Nay" like a tear, and pushed her cup a little from her without seeming to know it.

But Lorenzo had seen the act of repulsion, and he called over his shoulder to the waiter, who stood behind him watching Althea, "Haven't you got any cocoa?"

"Chocolate," said the waiter, impassively. "That do?"

Lorenzo saw Althea's face brighten, and he said, "Yee — yes, I *should* say," and then Althea and he laughed together at the joke that puzzled the waiter. They were very gay over their breakfast when he came back with the chocolate, though they were dashed a little at going when the same gloom that they had noticed in the sleeping-car porter fell upon their waiter, after Lorenzo had gathered up all the change he had brought them.

"What is it, Lorenzo, seems to come over them so at the last? He was so polite when we sat down, and took our bundles and everything, and he didn't even offer to hand them back when we left."

# IV

THEY were out on the sidewalk again, and were pushing aimlessly ahead under their burdens. The air felt fresher outside, and a breeze had begun to stir. "I don't know," said Lorenzo. "I guess they're rather changeable, that's all. Now, Althea, I can see that you're troubled about that dress of yours, and I want you should go into some of these stores with me and see if we can't match your sack better."

"Do you truly, Lorenzo?" she returned, in a flutter of pleasure. "Well!"

"Yee, I want to see you in something a little more seasonable. It's summer, and I'd like you to have — well, a white dress, I believe."

"But that wouldn't go any better with the sack than this one."

"Well, I guess we can find a sack that it *will* go with, then," said Lorenzo. "I always heard that they got married in white, anyway. I want you should look like other folks."

"Yee," Althea assented, a little faint with her

consciousness.

They passed a good many stores where there were dresses hanging at the doors or in the windows, but Lorenzo showed himself very fastidious; and though Althea thought some of them would do, he would only say that they could come back if they did not see anything that suited them better.

"I saw some dresses in a store under that big hotel down yonder a piece, and I want to ask about them first. Didn't you notice them?"

"Yee, I did. But isn't it rather of a fashionable place?"

"That's just what I'm looking for," said Lorenzo, and Althea laughed tremulously.

When they came down opposite the hotel he boldly led the way across the street, and would not let her falter at the shop door. "Now you come right in, Althea. I know more about the world-outside than you do," he said, in an imperative whisper.

He was blushing, too, though, when he set their things down on the floor, and a tall, handsome woman came flowingly forward to meet them, between counters gay with hats and bonnets, and clothes-trees with sacks and jackets, and figure-frames with gowns that swept the floor with silken trains. The shop-woman looked at them with a blush as bright as their own or brighter, but subdued to a softer effect by the film of powder that had got a little into her eyebrows.

She glanced inquiringly from one to the other, and at Althea's vain gasp she said to Lorenzo, as if he were an old man of the world, and they could understand each other perhaps better, "Is there something I could show madam?"

"Yee, there is," said Lorenzo. "We wanted to get some kind of a dress, if they a'n't all too dear."

"We have all prices," said the woman, and she touched different gowns as she spoke. "Seventy-five dollars, one fifty, sixty-two and a half, forty-five."

"You wanted something in cotton goods, didn't you, Althea?" asked Lorenzo, artfully, so as both to escape from the offer of these garments, which he did not wish to discredit by refusing them, and to bring Althea into the transaction.

"Yee, I did." And when Lorenzo whispered,

"*Yes* — don't say *yee*," she promptly retorted, in undertone, "*You* keep saying it too." And as if she had plucked up courage from inculpating him, she added to the shopwoman, "I should like something that would go with this sack and hat."

"Oh, well, then," said the shopwoman, as if she now understood exactly, and in a tone that transferred her allegiance instantly from Lorenzo to Althea, "I have something here very pretty and very cheap," and she took up from a heap of dainty dresses thrown across a table a frock of white muslin, trimmed with ends and knots of cherry ribbon, and fluttered over with lace and ruching and ruffling. "This is *very* cheap," she said, looking at the tag on it, and then drawing it over her arm with her right hand and holding it out to survey it with a glance of her sidelong head, in which there was an eye that studied both the young lovers. "It is quite a dream — and imported. It would fit you perfectly, madam. We're about at the end of our season for summer things now, and you could have this — it's marked thirty-five — for twenty-five."

Lorenzo stood agape, but Althea did not seem to know that he was even there. She was rapt in the ecstasy of the pretty dress. "Could — would you let me try it on first?"

"Why, certainly, madam. Just come with me."

Althea followed like one led by a spell. Lorenzo sat down on one of the revolving stools before a show-case filled with ribbons, with Althea's bags and parcels at his feet. It seemed to him that he sat there a long time. While he waited the shopwoman drifted in twice — once to fetch away a coquettish cape from one of the clothes-trees, and once to take a gauze hat from a peg. Then nothing happened for a time; and he had begun to wonder what was keeping Althea when he lifted his downcast eyes and beheld a vision.

It was Althea and it was not Althea. It was Althea as she would look, he suddenly thought, in the spirit-life, if spirits could be as beautiful as people on the earth, and have some of the danger in them. He could only deeply murmur, "Well, well!" and stare and stare.

"Will it do?" she entreated, with a smile that had a heavenly splendor in it.

He shut his mouth and swallowed, and then opened it again, but he could not speak.

"I think," said the shopwoman, "that madam looks superb in that dress, and she must have the cape with it. Her black sack is very nice, but it's a little out of style, and it's rather more of a spring and fall garment. Don't you think the hat is very becoming, too? The ribbon is the same as that on the dress." She touched a knot of it on the hat, and another knot of it on Althea's breast, and Lorenzo felt as if his own heart were under the place. "As the season is passing I can let you have them at the same reduction as the dress. I should have wanted twenty-five for the cape at the beginning of the month, and fifteen for the hat. You can have them both now for twenty-five — just fifty in all. And there isn't a stitch needed in any of them."

"They do seem to fit," said Lorenzo.

"She could wear them into the street this moment," said the woman.

Althea said nothing. She let her eyes fall.

"I guess we shall have to take them," said Lorenzo, and he got his pocket-book out.

Althea turned suddenly upon him. "Don't you do it unless you feel you'd ought to, Lorenzo. If it isn't right, I don't want you should do it."

"Oh, I guess it's all right," said Lorenzo, and the shopwoman confirmed him in the opinion.

"It would be simply wicked for madam not to have them."

"Yee, it *would!*" said Lorenzo more heartily, and he paid the bills over on the counter.

The woman took them with an absent air, as if she too were bewitched with the beauty she had adorned. "The hat would look ever so much better, of course," she said, "if madam's hair was the natural length. You must come back when it's grown out, and let me show you another."

It seemed a joke, and they laughed. Lorenzo said, boldly, "Yee, we will." And then he said, to help get away, "Well, Althea, I guess we must be going."

"Oh, then, madam will wear the things at once? Well, that is right. Where did you say I should send the old ones?"

The shopwoman addressed Lorenzo, and he blushed — he did not know why. "Well, we haven't gone to any hotel yet. Could — could we leave them here a little while?"

"Certainly, by all means," said the woman. "What name?"

"Well," said Lorenzo, and he thought a moment, "I guess you better just put Lorenzo Weaver on."

"Very well," said the shopwoman, and she wrote it down on a piece of paper which she pinned to the sack Friend Ella Shewall had lent Althea. In the midst of all that finery it now looked very common and shabby. Lorenzo said he would come round for the things a little later, and she said, politely, "Oh, any time!" and she followed them to the door. "I *wish*," she said," I could have seen madam with her hair long. It's such a pretty shade. Cut off in sickness, I suppose."

"Yee," said Lorenzo; and as they issued upon the sidewalk he was aware that Althea shrank from him, perhaps rather spiritually than corporeally, and yet really. "I know," he pleaded, "that I oughtn't to have said that, Althea, and I hated to do it as much as you would. But what could I do?"

"Nay, we seem to have to tell lies whenever folks speak to us," said Althea, sadly.

"Well, it a'n't lying exactly, or it a'n't so considered in the world-outside. It's considered just the same as putting folks off. I suppose we've got to conform in such things."

"Oh, yee," she sighed.

They walked along in an unhappy silence till Lorenzo said, "Those shoes, Althea, don't seem to go exactly with the rest." He looked down at the little feet which flatly patted the ground in the roomy gear of the Family.

She looked down at them too, and she assented in a rueful "Nay."

"I want to see if we can't find you something a little more like," he said; and he laughed to see a slight lift come at once into Althea's gait.

The young man in the shoe-store made Althea sit down for him to unlace her shoe, and then when he had put on the russet ties, which he said were the thing she wanted, felt her foot all over, to see that the fit was perfect, Lorenzo thought that they ought to have a woman for that, and he could see Althea blushing and shrinking, as if she thought so too; but he noticed another young woman trying on pair after pair of shoes under the same conditions, and he decided to say nothing about what was so plainly the custom of the world-outside. The shoes were certainly very pretty, and when Althea suffered him to see the points, the very sharp points of them, beyond her skirt, it seemed to him that her feet had gone to nothing in them. "A'n't they a little tight, Althea? No use getting shoes that will hurt you."

"They don't feel so," said Althea, conscientiously.

"You'll find more room in a sharp-pointed shoe, lady," said the shopman, ignoring Lorenzo in the matter, "than you will in a broad-pointed. Keep them on? All right. Where shall I send the old ones?"

Lorenzo explained, as he had to the modiste, that they had not got a hotel yet, and he asked if he might not call for the shoes later, and he had them marked with his name. "Seems to me you're a good deal taller than you were before, Althea," he said, when they were out on the sidewalk again.

"Yee; these shoes have got heels, and they seem to be pretty high." She no longer swung forward with the free gait he had always thought so beautiful, but walked mincingly, like the fashionably dressed ladies of the world-outside, whom they now began to meet more and more. He thought Althea was as well dressed as any of them, and he made her come into a gay little shop with him and choose a parasol. "Got to have something to keep the sun off, now your old bonnet's gone." And Althea laughed with him at the thought of it. She chose a white parasol with white silk fringe, and when the shopwoman suggested gloves she chose a pair of white ones, which the woman put on for her. Lorenzo bought her a lace handkerchief, and the woman showed her how to tuck it in at the waist of her dress, where she said handkerchiefs were worn now.

"Lorenzo," Althea said, with coquettish severity, when they were in the street again, "I'm not going another step with you unless you get something for yourself now."

"What do you want I should get?" he asked, fondly, with his heart in his throat.

"You ought to know," she returned, almost pertly.

"Well," said Lorenzo, "I been thinking I'd look full better in this hot weather with a straw hat."

"Yee, you would," said Althea; and they went into a men's furnishing store, where the shopman advised a straw hat with a very low crown and a very wide brim, and a deep ribbon with vertical stripes of red and blue. Lorenzo took it, and he took a necktie of white silk, which he was advised was the latest style, and he put it on at a little mirror in the back of the store. When he came forward with his new hat on a little slanted, he could see the glow of pride in his looks which came into Althea's face.

"Like it?" he asked. But it seemed as if she were too full to speak, and he resumed, carelessly, after he had given the shopman his name, and promised to call for his old hat and tie, "I don't know but we'd full as well go to some hotel now, Althea, and get our things sent there."

"Well, if you say so, Lorenzo," she answered, demurely.

"I declare, I don't know which one to go to, though," said Lorenzo. " We sha'n't be here often, I presume, and I should like to go to the very best; but if we asked anybody we shouldn't know whether they were right or not about it."

They stopped and stood looking up and down the street at the different hotels as they showed themselves in the perspective, but they could not make a choice.

"I wish we had asked that woman at the dress-store," said Lorenzo, dreamily; and Althea assented with an anxious, "Yee, she could have told."

"We might go and ask her now," said Lorenzo, "and yet I kind of hate to."

The driver of a gay, wood-colored surrey, who was slowly walking his horses up and down with an eye abroad for custom, placed his own interpretation on the wistful air of the young couple standing at the edge of the sidewalk and looking into the street. He pulled up beside them before they were aware. "Carriage? Take you to the Lake for a dollar! Drive?"

Lorenzo hastily whispered Althea, "We could ask *him* which is the best, on the way. And — and, Althea, we have got to ask somebody about a minister!" She questioned his meaning with her eyes, and he added, "To marry us."

She flushed and looked down, and admitted, faintly, "Yee."

"The driver could take us to a good one."

The driver waited patiently for the end of their conference, though they had not yet answered a word. He suggested, "Take you through the principal streets first, and not charge you anything more."

"I guess we better, Althea," said Lorenzo; and she let him help her into the surrey with a soft "Well."

# V

THE driver looked sharply round at them, and then turned about to his horses again. As he drove by the United States, and the Grand Union, and Congress Hall, and out past the Windsor, he named the different great hotels to them, and Lorenzo caught at the chance to ask him which was the best. "Well, I don't know as I could hardly make a choice between the four biggest. It depends on what you want for your money." He leaned half round, so as to converse with his passengers at his ease, and lightly controlled his slim sorrels with his left hand, while he stretched his right arm along the back of the seat. "If you want old-family business, I sh'd go to the States; and if you want all the earth can give in the way of solid comfort, I sh'd go to Congress Hall; and if you want something very tony, I sh'd go to the Windsor; but if you're in for all the life you can get, and all the distinguished visitors, and the big politicians, and style, and jewelry, and full band all the while, you want to go to the Grand Union. That's where *I'd* go if I was in Saratoga for a good time; but tastes differ, and there a'n't a word to say against the other big hotels, or any house in the place, as far as *I've* heard from 'em. Lady object to smokin'?" The driver suddenly addressed himself to Lorenzo. "Because if she don't, I'll finish my cigar." He spoke with the unlighted remnant of a cigar between his teeth.

Lorenzo looked at Althea, and she said, "Nay, I don't mind."

A smile ran up into the hard, averted cheek of the driver. He was a slim young fellow, who wore his straw hat at an impudent angle, and had a handsome face full of wicked wisdom; at the same time there was something like a struggle of conscience in the restraint from impertinence which he put upon himself. "If you'll just take these lines a second," he said, giving them into Lorenzo's hand; and then he lighted a match and exhaled his thanks with the first whiff of his cigar. "I can always talk so much better when I'm smokin', but I don't never like to smoke when my passengers object." He started up his horses briskly, and pointed out the objects of interest as he passed them. "That's Congress Park. You want to come here in the afternoon for the music — Troy band — and there's a balloon ascension there to-day; that's something you don't want to miss." He said, more especially for Althea's behoof, "Lady goes up." He let them look a moment at the pretty park with its stretch of level lawn, and its pavilion and kiosk, its fountain, and its amphitheatrical upland, with a roofage of darker and lighter green propped on tall pine and oak tree stems, and then he jerked his head towards a building on the left. "That's the Saratoga Club. Gamblin' place," he explained to their innocence. "Lots of money exchanges hands every night. German prince dropped ten thousand there one night, and he didn't take the whole night for it either. It's a gay place, if it *don't* look it." In fact, with its discreetly drawn curtains, its careful keeping of grass and flowers, the clubhouse looked in the bright morning sun like the demure dwelling of some rich man who did not care to flaunt his riches. "Indian encampment," said the driver, with another nod to the left, a little farther up the hill. "Get your fortune told there; shooting-gallery, Punch and Judy, and a little of everything." He nodded at a splendid villa on the right, with an auctioneer's sign upon it. "One of our leadin' gamblers' house. Cost him eighty thousand dollars, and won't bring twenty under the hammer. Got caught in the panic. Took to speculatin'. Been all right if he'd stuck to the cards," he concluded, as if this were the moral.

Lorenzo's mind worked with rustic slowness through a cloud of worldly ignorance, and the driver had time to point out several other notable residences on the handsome avenue which they were passing through, and told them that it was the way to the horse-races, and that they ought to be in Saratoga for the races, before Lorenzo could get round to ask, "But a'n't it against the law to gamble?"

"It's against the gospel too, I guess," said the driver, "but you wouldn't know it in Saratoga. It's the gamblin' and the racin' that makes the place." He spoke with that pride which people feel in their local evils if they are very great. He swept his passengers with his hardy eye, as if for full enjoyment of any horror he had raised in them, and ended: "And there a'n't but one single minister here that I ever heard of that's had the gall to say a word against hoss-racin'. That's what Saratoga is."

His point was lost to them in the thought that came into both their minds at once. Lorenzo whispered it : "Wouldn't that be the one?"

"I don't know," Althea began. Then she said, boldly, "Yee, it would. Ask who it is."

It took courage; but Lorenzo was leaning forward to put the question, when the driver turned round upon them and said, "But if it a'n't one thing it's another, and I don't suppose Saratoga's any worse than any other place *in the world-outside.*"

He pronounced the last words slowly, but with no apparent consciousness that they must have a peculiar effect with Lorenzo and Althea, who mutely shrank together at them. "You ought to let me fetch you here in the afternoon if you want to see life," the driver went on, carelessly. "It's a string of carriages going out one side, and a string coming in on the other. Or it is," he added, more candidly, "in the season. It's full early yet."

It was Althea who commanded herself first. When the danger of discovery seemed past

Lorenzo was still silent, but she began to talk and to ask the driver questions, which he answered, *"Yes,* ma'am," and *"No,* ma'am," with a crowing stress on the opening word that seemed personal to her at first, and then only personal to himself. But it was as if he had to be held in check continually from taking liberties, and it tasked all the severity Althea had learned in teaching the girls' school at the Family to manage him. Lorenzo was no help to her; but she held her own, even upon ground so strange to her.

When they reached the wayside restaurant at the end of the lake, he said, Well, here they were, if they wanted to get a lemonade or anything; and he added to Lorenzo, "Be a dollar; I sha'n't charge you anything extra for showin' you round first, as I *said.*"

"I thought," said Lorenzo to Althea, as they followed, passively, the lead of the waiter who was showing them to a table on the veranda of the house, "that it meant taking us back, too. Didn't you, Althea?"

"Yee," Althea whispered, in return. "But I'm glad it didn't. I don't believe I like him very much. We can take another carriage back."

"Oh yee."

They could see far up the lovely lake, from their table, and beyond a stretch of level the noble range of nearer uplands and farther mountains that frames the Saratoga landscape on the northward.

"It's sightly, Althea," Lorenzo murmured: and she answered in the same undertone, "Yee, it is."

She spoke vaguely, for she was noticing the people who were sitting about at the other tables, and trying to make out what kind of people they were. There was one group of rather noisy girls, who had very yellow hair and bright cheeks, and who seemed to her like a bevy of harsh, brilliant birds; their eyes shone glassily when they turned to look at her. A family party of father and mother, and children who had to be constantly checked and controlled were at another table. At another still a pair in later-middle life, who sat at their half-eaten ices, seemed to be studying the rest, and Althea could feel that Lorenzo and she were peculiarly interesting to this pair.

"They are talking about us," she said to Lorenzo.

"Well," he returned, after a long draught of his lemonade — he had ordered that because the driver had mentioned lemonade — "they can't say anything against *you*, Althea."

"I wonder if they live in Saratoga," she said.

"What makes you ask that?"

"I don't know," she answered, faintly, and she looked down. "Don't you think they are very nice appearing?"

"Yee, I do," said Lorenzo, after a moment. "We've got to ask somebody about a minister, I presume," he mused aloud, "sooner or later."

A quick red and white dyed and then blanched Althea's face. "There's no — hurry. I like keeping *so*, don't you, Lorenzo?"

"Oh yee. But we can't keep so always."

"Nay."

"I do declare, when that fellow spoke up so about the world-outside I didn't know which way to look. Althea, if you think those friends reside here, and it would do to ask *them* about a minister —"

"Nay," she whispered back in a sudden panic, "you mustn't!"

"Well, I won't then."

They had to pass the elderly couple in going out, and Althea heard the gentleman say to the lady: "It's quite the nun look."

"Yes. I don't understand," the lady answered. "Beautiful — lovely — pure! It's like a child's — an angel's."

They were both looking up the lake, where the little excursion steamer was coming in sight.

# VI

LORENZO and Althea found a number of carriages standing outside, but the drivers all said they were engaged. The driver who had brought them was sitting under a tree smoking. He waited for them to ask the others, and then he called out briskly to them, as if he had never seen them before, "Carriage?"

They looked at each other. "It would be too far to walk back," Lorenzo suggested.

"It would dust this dress," said Althea, "and I can't seem to walk so well in these shoes."

Lorenzo turned to the driver, who had now come up to them. "What will you charge to take us back to town?"

The driver reflected. "Well, I've got to go back pretty soon anyway. I'll leave it to you."

"If it was worth a dollar to bring us here," said Lorenzo, firmly, "it's worth a dollar to take us back; and it a'n't worth any more."

"All right," said the man, and he jumped to his

seat. "Where do you want I should leave you?" he asked, turning round to them when they were seated, while his sorrels started gayly off of themselves. "Leave you at Congress Park, if you say so. It's central, and you could set down in there, and think what you wanted to do next."

They felt an impertinence in his suggestion, but it expressed their minds, and Lorenzo assented with a stiff "All right." He received some remarks of the driver's so forbiddingly that he left them quite to themselves until they reached the park.

When they dismounted at the upper gate he took Lorenzo's dollar with a certain hesitation. "I don't know as I'd ought to charge you so much for just bringin' you back." He looked at them, and then suddenly turned upon Lorenzo: "Say, a'n't you up from Lebanon? You're Shakers, anyway!"

"Nay," returned Lorenzo, angrily, "we are *not.*"

"Nays have it," said the young fellow. Without looking round at them, he hollowed out his hands about the match he struck, and lighted a cigar at it while he drove up the street at a slow walk, with the lines held between his knees.

"Oh, Lorenzo," cried Althea, "we *are*! You *know* we are! How could you say it?"

"Well, Althea, we *a'n't* from Lebanon!"

"Oh, you know it wasn't that you denied. We *are* Shakers. Run after him — run after him, and tell him so, no matter what happens!"

"Well, well! But just as you say, Althea. I don't want to tell a lie any more than you do."

Lorenzo started and ran up the street after the carriage, calling out, "Say! hello! Stop there a minute!" The driver stopped and looked round. Lorenzo did not give himself time to falter after he came up. "We *are* Shakers. Yee, we are! What is it to you?" he added, in defiance.

"Oh, nothing," said the young fellow. "I'm from down around Lebanon myself. Been at the Family there many a time. Just wanted to see if you'd lie about it; always heard a Shaker wouldn't lie."

"Well, we're *not* from Lebanon!" Lorenzo retorted, with futile resentment.

"All right," said the driver. "Lookin' for a minister?"

The answer seemed to fly out of Lorenzo's mouth of itself: "Yee, we are."

"I thought so," said the driver. "Well, I know the whitest man in *this* town, and I can take you to him if you want to get married. Take you and the lady there, and it sha'n't cost you a cent. Say!" He drew from his waistcoat-pocket the dollar bill which Lorenzo had just given him, and handed it to him. "You just take that, and if he a'n't all I tell you, you *keep* it. I don't want any man's money without I earn it."

"All right," said Lorenzo, and he put the bill in his pocket and walked back to Althea in a kind of daze, while the carriage slowly followed. "Althea, he says *he* knows a good minister."

"Get right in, lady," said the driver. "If you're all right, I guess you won't feel but what *he* is. Well, I'll tell you what! He's the one — and he's the only one — that's got the gall to preach against hoss-racin'."

He looked as if his words must carry conviction; the lovers were helpless before them, and they mounted to the place they had so lately left. The driver turned reassuringly to Althea again. "Now don't you be anxious any. If you don't like his looks you just come right out again, and I'll take you anywheres else you want to go — and

I know every minister in the place — and no extra charge."

They had not even to go inside for the test the driver proposed. The minister himself answered Lorenzo's ring; he pushed open the lattice door that opened outwardly, and scanned them from the threshold with a face that seemed kind and gentle as well as shrewd. Lorenzo and Althea looked at each other without being able to speak.

The driver spoke for them from his carriage, where he waited to see whether they should find the minister at home. "*Good*-morning, dominie! I want you to take care of these folks. Friends of mine."

The minister looked up at him from under brows that frowned in the strong sunlight, and then laughed in recognition. "I hope they have some better recommendation. Will you walk in?" he asked of the young couple, and he held the door open for them to enter, and shut it upon them in the cool, dark entry, without further notice of the driver. Then he led them into a dim parlor, and when he had made a little more light in it by turning the slats of one of the blinds, he asked them if they would not sit down. He said he would be with them in a moment, and he went out, as if to still the clamor of children's voices which made themselves heard from the rear of the house, and then were silent.

# VII

ALTHEA clutched Lorenzo nervously by the coat-sleeve in the twilight of the parlor, and whispered, "Oh, Lorenzo, do you think we'd better?"

"Yee, I do, Althea. It would be ridic'lous to back out now. We've got to do it."

"Yee, I presume we have. But not — not unless you wish it as much as ever you did!"

"I do, full as much. Don't you, Althea?"

"Oh, yee — yee. Will it take — very long?"

"How should I know, Althea?"

"That is so. But I hope it won't take long. I can't seem to — get my — breath."

"Now, Althea —"

"There! There he is! I shall *behave*, Lorenzo. But don't you — don't you *try* to deny anything if he asks you!"

"Nay, I won't, Althea."

The minister came in again, and Althea saw that he had a different coat on and a book in his hand. He sat down and faced them, gravely smiling, and pushed softly backward and forward in the rocking-chair he had taken. After waiting for them to speak, he asked, "Is there something I can do for you?"

He looked at Lorenzo, who glanced in turn at Althea; she met his eye with a mute reproach that made him speak.

"Yee, there is. We — we some thought of gettin' — married."

"Well," said the minister, still smiling, "that is rather serious business, though people seem not to think so always. Do you live in this state?"

"Nay — or no, I *should* say. We are from Massachusetts."

"Have you friends in Saratoga whom you would like to have present?"

"Nay, we are strangers here," answered Lorenzo. "We just came this morning." He looked at Althea for the reward of his honesty, but her eyes were fixed upon the minister.

"At all in a hurry?" asked the minister, with a smile.

"Some of a hurry," Lorenzo asserted, and he drew a long, sighing breath, as if to strengthen himself for further question.

The minister laughed a little. He was a tall,

fair young man, with a light-colored mustache cut short along his lip. "I'm sorry for the hurry. I don't think it's the best way to get married. But if you've made up your minds —"

"Yee — yes, we have," said Lorenzo, boldly. "Haven't we, Althea?"

"Yee," Althea answered, more faintly.

"It a'n't any new thing or any sudden thing with us," said Lorenzo. "We've thought it over, and we've talked it over, and we've made up our minds, fully. The only hurry that there's been about it was our comin' here, and that we *had* to do, to save feelin', as much as anything. We no *need* to do it."

Still Althea did not look at Lorenzo, but at a favorable change that passed over the minister's face she gave a little sigh of relief.

"Well, that's good," said the minister. "I can marry you, of course, and I will, if you wish. But the step you are going to take is the most important step you can take in your whole lives. I like to have people realize that, before I help them to take it, and reflect that it is irrevocable. But if you are attached to each other you will wish it to be so," he suggested, always smiling.

"Yee," said Lorenzo.

"That is the theory," continued the minister, and he looked at Althea, as if he felt that he could address a finer and higher intelligence in her. "But the strongest feeling is not always the surest guide. Would you like to go away for a little while, and ask yourselves and each other whether you are quite sure, and then come back?" He looked from one to the other kindly. Althea glanced at Lorenzo as if shaken. Lorenzo would not meet her eye.

"We've done that already. We know our minds now as well as we ever shall," he said, with a kind of doggedness.

"Very well," said the minister. "I thought I ought to suggest it. I must ask whether there is anything in the lives of either of you, or in your circumstances, which should cause you a conscientious scruple against entering the state of marriage."

"Nay," they answered together.

"I needn't ask if you have either of you been married before or are now married?"

"Oh, nay," they answered, and Lorenzo permitted himself the relief of a laugh at the notion.

Althea smiled in sympathy.

"And your name?"

"Lorenzo Weaver."

"The lady's?"

"Althea Brown."

The minister made a note of the names, and he said, "Is that driver a friend of yours?"

"Nay," said Lorenzo, "we don't know him."

The minister laughed as if he enjoyed the rogue's pretence of intimacy with them. "Well," he said, "I don't see why we shouldn't proceed. As you have no friends of your own to be present, I will just call my wife to witness the ceremony."

He went out again, and Althea murmured to Lorenzo in the twilight, " Oh, I hope she'll come soon!"

"I don't believe but what she will," he murmured back. He tried to take her hand, to reassure her, but she kept it from him.

"Because if she don't," she scarcely more than gasped, "I don't believe I can bear it."

Lorenzo was silent, as if he did not know what to answer, and they sat mute together in the dim room till the minister came back.

"My wife will be in directly," he said, seating

himself in the rocking-chair; "she has to make some change in her dress;" and now he spoke to Althea more especially. "With you ladies everything in life seems an occasion for that."

He smiled, and Althea smiled in mechanical response. "Yee," she said.

The minister looked at her, and after a momentary hesitation he said, "May I ask why you use that form of speech. I notice that you both use it."

Althea looked at Lorenzo, and he answered, bluntly, "We are Shakers."

"Oh, indeed!" said the minister. "That is very interesting. I have never met any of your people before. You must excuse me if I say that I observed something peculiar in you at the first glance. But I supposed that the Shakers had a dress of their own."

"Yee, we have — in the Family," said Lorenzo; "but we got these things since we came into the world-outside."

The minister said "Oh!" and Althea blushed with a consciousness that imparted itself to the whole texture of her pretty dress, and to the cherry ribbons on her breast and hat. "But don't you use the plain language, and say thee and thou, like the Quakers?"

"Nay, we say Yee and Nay, 'for more than this cometh of evil.' "

A sort of sectarian self-satisfaction, a survival of conditions he had abandoned, expressed itself in Lorenzo's tone, and he was not apparently sensible of the irony in the minister's "Oh, I see!" But Althea stirred as if she felt it.

"We only say so now," she explained, "because we have the habit of it. We have no right to set ourselves above anybody else in the world-outside any more, as far as that goes."

"Will you excuse me?" said the minister, with a burst of frankness. "But if it isn't intrusive, I should like very much to know something about your Family life. You are communists, I believe?"

"Yee, we have all things common. There is not much to tell you. We all work and serve. I taught the school. Lorenzo was in the herb and seed shop; we put them up for sale."

"But your religious life — your social life?"

"We believe in the Bible, but we believe that Ann Lee came after Jesus to fulfill his mission. We think that revelation continues to this day, and that we are always in communion with the spirit world. The spirits give us our hymns and our music."

"I have heard something about it," said the minister, "and about your dancing at your meetings."

Lorenzo laughed with a little sectarian scorn. "That is about all that some folks in the world-outside think there is to it. That's what they come to see, generally. And it a'n't dancin', to call it rightly. It's more of a march."

"I should like to see it," said the minister. "But your distinctive social peculiarities besides your communism?"

Neither of the young people answered at once. At last Althea said, in a low voice, "We live the angelic life."

"What do you mean by that?"

She was silent, and looked at Lorenzo. He answered, impatiently, "They don't get married; they think they are as the angels in heaven."

"Oh, indeed! Then —"

"That's the reason we left them. If there had been any other way —" Lorenzo hesitated, and Althea took the word.

"We never should have left the Family as long as we lived. They took us when we were little, and they have taken care of us, and taught us, and done everything for us. They loved us, and we loved them. But —"

She stopped in her turn, and Lorenzo resumed, "Well, the whole story is, we got to feelin' foolish about each other."

"Do you mean," and the minister suppressed a smile as he spoke, "that you fell in love?"

"Well, I presume you would call it that in the world-outside."

"I see," said the minister. "And as you could not be married there —"

"Yee."

They were all silent now till Althea asked, in a trembling voice, "Do you think — it is wrong for us to — get married?"

The minister roused himself from the muse he was falling into. "Not the least in the world! Why should I think so?"

"We tried to look at it in every light, but sometimes I am afraid we were blinded by our feelings for each other. We didn't wish to be selfish about it, and it did seem as if our —"

"Being in love?" suggested the minister.

"Yee — was a kind of leading, and that we had as good a right to think that it was put into our hearts as any of the other things."

"That is the way the world-outside regards it," said the minister, with a smile that betrayed his relish of the phrase he had adopted. "We even go so far as to say that matches are made in heaven. I must confess that some of them don't seem to bear out the theory."

"But you think — you think that there is nothing wrong in marriage itself, even if folks are not always happy in it?" Althea pursued.

"Most certainly," said the minister. "It's often very bad; but at its worst it's probably always the best thing under the circumstances." He seemed to speak in earnest, but he kept his smile on Althea, as if her quaint seriousness amused him in its relation to the worldly gayety of her appearance. The spirit of a nun speaking from the fashions that Althea wore with as much grace as if she were born in them might well have appealed to a less imaginative sympathy. "Why do you ask? Were you taught that it was wrong in itself?"

"Nay — nay," she faltered.

"They're always talkin' against it," said Lorenzo, bitterly. "They say themselves that it's all right in the earthly order; and yet they keep braggin' up the gospel relation and the angelic life, and tellin' you that Christ never got married; and I think it's wore on her. I tried to convince her the best I could that Christ wouldn't have gone to weddin's if he hadn't approved of 'em, for all he didn't marry."

"Do you think he did approve of them?" she entreated, tremulously, of the minister.

"I think he did, indeed."

"But if — Don't his not marrying make it appear as if he thought it was of the earthly order?"

"There it is again!" cried Lorenzo. "She can't seem to get past that! I tell her — and I don't know how many times I've told her that we can't all expect to lead the angelic life in this world."

"We can if we choose," she retorted, nervously, speaking to Lorenzo, but still intent upon the minister's face.

"I don't believe," he said, "that we ought to study a literal conformity to the life of Jesus in everything; that is, we should not make his practice in such a matter an article of faith. I should say that if any one felt strongly appealed to by it, he would do well to follow it; but if he did not, he would not do well to follow it; and especially would not do well to enforce it upon others."

"There! Didn't I say so?" demanded Lorenzo of Althea. "Let everybody do according to his own conscience."

"As long," said the minister, "as Christ's words do not explicitly condemn marriage —"

The voice of Althea broke in upon him, still tremulous but clear, and gaining firmness to the close: "And Jesus answering said unto them, the children of this world marry and are given in marriage; but they which shall be accounted worthy to obtain that world and the resurrection from the dead neither marry nor are given in marriage; neither can they die any more; for they are equal unto the angels; and are the children of God, being the children of the resurrection."

The minister listened with a smile, as if her child-like fanaticism interested him like something of rare and peculiar quality, but he replied, with a certain touch of compassionate respect, "Is that the passage they ground their doctrine on? You know those are Luke's words, and Luke had his facts at second-hand. The other gospels do not report the words of Jesus so, but even if Luke's report were the most accurate, as it's certainly the fullest, I should not take it literally. I have thought a good deal about that passage," said the minister, "for I have to do a good deal of marrying and giving in marriage, and I read in it a deeper meaning than the face of the words bear. In a certain sense, marriage is both the death and the resurrection. If you will think about it, you will see that it is the very symbol of eternity in human life. All other human relations dissolve and end, but that endures imperishably. The family continually perishes through marriage, which creates it. Children are born to a wedded pair, and there is a family; they grow up and marry, and the family which they constituted ceases to be, as the family which their children shall constitute will cease to be. But the marriage of the father and mother remains to all eternity. If there is no giving in marriage beyond this life it is not in condemnation of marriage, but in recognition of the fact that it is *from* everlasting as well as *to* everlasting, like all things eternal."

"There, Althea," murmured Lorenzo; but the girl did not speak.

The minister went on, "The husband and the wife lay down their separate lives, and take up a joint life, which, if they are truly married, shall be theirs forever. There is no marrying after death, but heaven is imaged in every true marriage on earth; for heaven is nothing but the joy of self-giving, and marriage is the supreme self-giving. We call the *ceremony* 'getting married,' he pursued, expanding with a certain pleasure in his theme, which was not, perhaps, very relevant to it; "but the living together, the adjustment of temperaments, the compromise of opinions, the reconciliation of tastes, is what we *should* call 'getting married.' I should wish you to remember that *marriage is the giving up of self.* That is its highest meaning. If it is not that, it is something so low as to be the unworthiest of all human relations. If you do not give up yourselves, if you insist upon what you think your rights against one another, you will be yokemates of perdition, and your marriage will be a hell. I suppose it is the dread of something like this in marriage that has created the celibate sects in all times and in all religions. But marriage is properly the death of the individual, and in its resurrection you will rise not as man and woman, but as one pair, in the unity of immortal love. I declare," he broke off, "I don't know what's keeping my wife. I'm detaining you an unconscionable time. If you'll excuse me, I'll just go —" He started from his chair, and made a movement towards the door.

Althea sprang to her feet, and put out her hand. "Nay!" she said, nervously, "don't call her yet. Lorenzo — I — Don't you believe we'd better take a little time to think — and come back? You could let us come back?" she entreated of the minister.

"Why, surely! Again and again, as often as you wish. Go and think it over; and if you still have any misgiving —"

"We haven't any misgivings," said Lorenzo, stoutly. "But if she wants to get her mind clear, I won't be the one to hinder or hurry her."

"That is the right spirit," said the minister, and he offered the young fellow his hand. "I shall be here till twelve o'clock — it's eleven now — and after that not till between four and five. I shall be glad to see you back, but if you don't come — Good-morning!" He smiled cordially upon them at the lattice door, where he parted from them, and held it open for them to pass out.

# VIII

THEY blinked in the strong sunshine, and walked dizzily down the bit of brick pavement to the gate, and then down the quiet street.

"I don't know what you'll say to me, Lorenzo," Althea began.

Without looking round at her he answered, "You done right, Althea."

"Oh, do you think so?" she quavered. "I did for the best; I thought we ought to talk it over more, and look into our minds and ask ourselves — I'm not sure that I see all these things in the light he did."

"Seemed to me he gave us a pretty solemn talk," said Lorenzo — "more than he'd any need to. Well, he said as much himself; I a'n't criticisin' him. I thought we had our minds made up. But I could see how he unsettled you by some of the things he said, and if you don't think he made it out so very clear, after all, I want you should feel just right about it every way, Althea. We can come back this afternoon."

"Lorenzo, if you say so, we will go back now — this minute!" she cried, passionately. "I didn't draw back on my account any more than yours."

"Nay, we'll wait now awhile — or, any rate, till we see it in the right light. But I'll tell you what, Althea: I think we've thought enough about it, and more than enough. What we want to do now is to think of something else, and let our marryin' alone awhile. It's like this, the way I view it it's like a sum that you can't do or work out anyhow; and you can beat yourself against it all day, and you can't do it. But let it alone a spell, and come back after your mind's rested, and you'll find it's done itself."

"I do believe it's so, Lorenzo," said Althea, with a potential joy in her tone.

"Yee. And, Althea, I say, let's forget all about it, and go round and enjoy ourselves. It's about as fine a day as I ever saw, and it a'n't likely we shall be back in Saratoga very soon again. There's no use makin' a poor mouth, and I don't see as there's any reason. You was feelin' well enough before we went in there, and I guess nothing's really happened to make us downhearted."

He leaned over from his loftier height with a

smile, and his shoulder touched hers. At the contact her hand glided out upon his arm, as if without her will, and rested there. She did not answer, but in a moment she halted him with a little pull. "Where are we going?"

He looked round and laughed. "Well, well! I declare if I thought. I guess we came down the street because it was easier than to go up."

"I hope that isn't going to be the way with us through life!" she said, and she looked round with a laughing face.

A young man driving a pair of light sorrels in a wood-colored surrey drew up in the middle of the road, and held his whip towards them. "Carriage?" he called out.

"Nay, we don't want to ride," Lorenzo began.

"Well, then," said the driver, and he guided his team closer to them on the corner where they stood, "I guess I shall have to get that dollar from you." He smiled benignly at the bewildered look Lorenzo gave him, and then laughed at his dawning consciousness.

"Well, well! I forgot all about it!" Lorenzo put his hand in his pocket, while Althea drew her hand from his arm; he took out the note and handed it to the driver.

"Dominie made it all right for you, then?"

Lorenzo tried to withdraw with dignity from the confidential ground taken with him. "I guess so," he said, with dry evasion.

"Well, I thought so," the driver exulted, "when you come out; and when I see her take your arm, I knowed there wasn't a doubt about it. Say, why don't you get in and let me take you to your hotel? It sha'n't cost you a cent. You want to pull up at the Grand Union in style, if that's where you're goin'."

Althea shrank in dismay from these preternatural intuitions, but it seemed to Lorenzo, though he felt her reluctance, that it would be better to accept the offer, and get rid of the fellow at the hotel door. He was afraid that otherwise he might follow them the whole way, and perhaps give a mortifying publicity to their adventure by trying to talk with them about it from the middle of the street. Besides, he did not know where the Grand Union was, and it seemed settled that they were to go there.

"I guess we better, Althea," he suggested.

"Well, if you say so, Lorenzo."

"Well, that's right! Get right in," said the driver. When they were seated and he turned about to arrange the linen lap-cloth over their knees, he laughed, for Althea's pleasure, and said, "'Now you're married, you must obey, and mind your husband night and day,' as the song says. Well, that's the way it works for a while, anyhow. Then it's the husband's turn, and *he* takes a hack at obeyin'. Well, it's all in a lifetime, as I tell my wife. Didn't think I was married? How did you suppose I was on to you so quick? Been there myself. Got the nicest little wife in *this* town. But I guess I should ha' known what you was after, anyway. Lots o' couples come to Saratoga to get married in a hurry. It's all right! Did the dominie ask you some hard questions? He does oftentimes, and if he can't feel just right about it, he won't splice you. I've had to take more than one couple to another shop. But he's all right, the dominie is! Tell him what you was?"

"We no need to feel ashamed of anything," said Lorenzo, resentfully.

"Well, that's so. That's what the dominie likes. I could tell you some pretty tough stories about the couples I've had to hunt round for a minister with."

Lorenzo wished to say something that would put a stop to the fellow's talk, but Althea pressed his arm as a sign for him not to answer, and he forbore.

The driver seemed to interpret their silence aright. "Well," he said, "it's a pleasure to strike the right sort of couple, and I guess that's what the dominie thought too. He's all right. Didn't I tell you he was a white man? Well, he *is*." Though his words ran so freely, the driver suffered from a poverty of ideas which now seemed to make itself apparent even to himself, and he fell silent before they reached the hotel. "Here we are," he said, when he pulled up in front of it at last.

Lorenzo and Althea sat staring at the great hostelry's facade, with the upward sweep of its portico in front of them, the wide stretch of its verandas southward, and northward the glitter of the shops and offices under it. Men were going and coming up and down the steps of the portico, and they thronged the office within, and stretched in groups along the verandas, with their feet on the railing; they were smoking and talking together. Here and there one sat alone, with his cigar sloped upward and his hat-brim sloped downward almost to the point of meeting.

There were very few women to be seen, and Lorenzo hesitated, with a glance at Althea. The driver tried to encourage him.

"You want to go right through the inside piazza, and get the rest of the concert; it a'n't over yet. And you can register just as well afterwards; you won't have any trouble about rooms so early in the season." They dismounted anxiously, and stood looking up into the hotel. "There!" said the driver. "I guess *they're* goin' in. You just follow them, and you'll be all right." He pointed at a group of ladies who were mounting the steps, and then drove away. The ladies pushed fearlessly into the hotel, and Althea followed with Lorenzo. The place was full of men talking and smoking, like those outside, and she missed the shelter of the deep Shaker bonnet where she could have hid her face from the glances that seemed to seek it from all sides. She knew that her cropped hair must look strange under her gay hat, and she wanted to ask Lorenzo whether it looked so *very* strange; but he was intent upon finding a way between the groups and keeping those ladies in sight. The noise of shuffling feet and rippling dresses confused her, and the vastness of the place awed her; through a doorway on one hand she caught a glimpse of a long room with splendors of upholstery and furnishing, under shining chandeliers and deep mirrors; and then suddenly they reached a wide open doorway, and at the same moment there burst through upon them a joyous tide of music that seemed to Althea almost to sweep her from her feet, and made her cling closer to Lorenzo.

On either side of the doorway beautifully dressed women sat listening, or whispered with the haughty-looking men beside them, and before her tall, slim pines shot up from the levels of a wide lawn, and a fountain, set round with broad-leaved plants, gushed into the sunshine that their boughs sifted upon it. On the pathways that intersected each other under the trees nearer and farther pairs of young men and women strayed together to the limits of the high, many-windowed walls that enclosed the landscape.

"Lorenzo, Lorenzo!" she murmured, as they

found places among the company that they seemed to be an accepted part of, "do you believe that we're awake?"

"Yee, I guess we are at last, Althea. Do you like it?" he whispered back, with a lover's pleasure in her pleasure; he involuntarily took credit for it as if he had created it.

"I feel as if I had just come to life," she whispered. "Oh, how could it all have been, and we not know it!"

"I guess," he exulted, "there are a good many things in the world-outside that are never heard of in the Family. Do you feel *now* as if it was wrong?"

She saw the same look in his eyes that she knew he saw in hers. "Nay, that's all gone. I shall never think so any more."

Her hand found his at their side, and they sat with their fingers knitted together in the shelter of her drapery that flowed over them. The music that thrilled from the viols and violins, and breathed cool and piercing from the flutes and flageolets, seemed to claim Althea for the earth, and to fill her heart with a bliss of living. It liberated her from the fear that had been lurking in the bottom of her heart. It silenced that dull nether ache of doubt; it flattered and promised; it lured her out of the prison of herself, and invited her to be of its own ecstasy.

# IX

WHEN the piece ended a sweet, high pipe of a voice behind them said, "Won't you have a programme?" and Althea was aware of a little white hand dangling a printed leaf at her shoulder. She looked round and confronted a young girl, with bright, joyful eyes, and a smile of radiant happiness on her lips; she was very fair, with hair of pale yellow, which loosed itself from the mass in rings and tendrils at her temples and about her neck, and sunnily misted her uncovered head. She wore a light-blue dress, and in her lap lay a hat of yellow straw, with blue cornflowers knotted among its ribbons. "Mamma has one," she explained to Althea's look of question and reluctance, "and we don't need them both;" and she glanced at the elder lady in black beside her, who nodded a silent assent.

Althea took the programme provisionally, with some halting thanks, and the girl showed, with a deeply jewelled finger, where the musicians had got in it. She included Lorenzo, who was looking round at her, too, in the same hospitable smile. At the end of the next piece Althea offered to restore the programme, but she made her keep it, and she began to talk to her. She asked her if she did not think the music was too lovely for anything, and whether she had heard the music at the other hotels. She contended that it did not sound half so well there, and that it was everything to hear it in such a beautiful place. She asked Althea if she ever saw such a beautiful place, and she said that she did not believe that there was such a beautiful place anywhere. She made her look at the fountain, and while Althea was looking at it she knew the girl was looking at her hat and her dress.

At the end of the second piece she seemed to have gone much further with Althea in her mind. She leaned forward to ask, "Don't you just *love* Saratoga? We've been here a week, and I don't believe we can ever get enough of it. You won't mind my talking to you, will you, without being introduced? When you came through the door, I said to mamma, 'Well, there's *one* person that I have simply *got* to know; and when you came and sat down right in front of us, it did seem too much! Of course it must seem very un-ceremonious, and I shouldn't do so to every one. Do you mind?"

Althea contrived to get in that she did not, between this question and the next, but the girl seemed not to care much for her answers. "Have you ever been in Saratoga before? I think every-thing is so romantic here, and *perfect*. We didn't expect to stay so long, but" — she put on a sud-den state as she said so — "we've been detained by business. My husband had to go back to New York on business. He's with Stroud & Malkim there." She looked at Althea as if for an effect of the firm's name upon her, and added, "Curtains, you know. We did intend to go up to Lake George and Lake Champlain and to Montreal, but I shouldn't care if we spent every bit of the time in Saratoga. Are you staying in this hotel?"

Althea looked at Lorenzo. "Yee–es. We are go-ing to as soon as —"

The music began again; it was the last piece, and when it ended most of the people about them rose and dispersed; but certain of them waited till they could get away without being crowded, and her new friend leaned forward to advise Althea to wait till the jam was over.

Lorenzo said, "I guess you better, Althea, and I might as well go and register. I won't be gone but a little while, and if you'll stay right here I can easily find you again."

"Just as you say, Lorenzo," said Althea, but she looked up at him a little wistfully.

"Oh, we'll chaperon her!" cried their new friend, gayly; and as soon as Lorenzo left his chair she laid her hat upon her own, and slipped into the place next Althea. "Now you needn't tell me if you don't want to, but I just *know* you're on your wedding journey! When you first came in, arm in arm, I told mamma I *bet* you were." She curled her lip in over her teeth, and questioned Althea with her gay eyes; then she flashed out: "You *are*, I know it! Oh, I *wish* George was here! George — that's *my* husband, and he's the *nicest* fellow! Well, I wish you could see him; he'll be here to-night, too. I should like our husbands to get acquainted. I think yours is awfully nice-looking; he ought to have a mustache; he would look splendid in a mustache. I tell George *his* mustache is too big for anything. There he is!" She pulled a little watch from her belt, and sprung it open; on the inside of the case was the head of a young man, which filled it so full that the ends of his mustache extended invisibly into space beyond it. "Don't you think he's good-looking?"

"Yee, I do," said Althea; but she did not think him so good-looking as Lorenzo.

The young wife did not wait for an answer; she pressed the pictured face to her lips, snapped the case to, and tucked the watch back in her belt. "It's taken right on the case; they do that now, and it's so much nicer than pasting the photograph. George gave it to me before we were married. Well, he had to hurry up; we didn't have a very long courtship. We got acquainted on the cars, and he said that the minute he set eyes on me he knew I was the girl he was going to marry. It was a perfect novel, from beginning to end; and I don't care what they say, but I know that the course of true love *does* run smooth, sometimes. It didn't have a single hitch with us ; but I *didn't* suppose we should be separated this way, right in the first week of our honeymoon. George says it's good practice, though; he's got to be on the road so much; and I've got to be left with mamma, and I might us well begin early; I've almost talked her to death about him already." She seemed to be reminded to look round for her mother; the older woman had made her escape for the moment. "Oh, there she is, by the fountain. She's just as fond of George as I am, and she's going to live with us when we get our flat in New York; we're going to board awhile first. Is your husband travelling?" She had to explain that her own husband went about over the country getting orders for the house of Stroud & Malkim, and she apparently forgot what she asked, for she followed her question up with another, not waiting for an answer. "Have you been to any of the stores in Saratoga yet? They have lovely things, and *so* cheap." She looked hard at Althea's costume.

"I got this dress and hat here this morning," Althea said.

The other clapped her hands. "I just *told* mamma you did! Did you get them at that place under the hotel, a little way up?"

"I guess so," Althea assented. "I didn't notice exactly."

"Well, if I ever knew anything like it! I do

believe it's the very dress George and I looked at yesterday, and I *know* I saw that hat in the window. They're real imported, the woman said, and they're *dreams,* both of them. George would have got them for me if they'd been my style. They're killing on you."

# X

LORENZO found himself before the great hotel register, which one of the clerks had wheeled round towards him. When he had fancied inscribing himself and Althea as Lorenzo Weaver and Wife, it had been very simple; but it suddenly came to him that they were not married, and that he could not truthfully call her his wife. He stood leaning over the register, and he was aware of the clerk waiting impatiently. He had said that he wished to register, and he was not doing so.

The clerk said severely, and, Lorenzo felt, disdainfully, "Let this gentleman register, please," and then he was aware of some one standing behind him. A large, flourishing-sort-of-looking man, with a shawl on his arm and a bag in his hand, which he put down when Lorenzo moved aside, wrote with the pen which the clerk dipped into the ink and offered him, "J. M. Bayne and Lady," in a rapid, authoritative hand, and the clerk said, "Room, Mr. Bayne?" And the man answered, "No; dinner. We're going on to Lake George in the afternoon. Like to check the things." And the clerk answered, "Opposite desk, please." And a black call-boy ran up and took the shawl and bag, and the man went away, and left Lorenzo to the register again. The man had solved the problem for him, and he wrote "Lorenzo Weaver and Lady." If Althea was not his wife, she was certainly, in the parlance of the world-outside, a lady, and this seemed a safe way out of the trouble.

"Dinner?" asked the clerk, who came back to him when he looked up from the register.

"Nay — no, I guess I will have a room. But we do want dinner," said Lorenzo. At the word he was sensible of being hungry.

The clerk wrote a number and an initial against Lorenzo's name, and then he asked, "Baggage?"

"What?" said Lorenzo.

"Any trunks or traps to go to your room?"

"Oh, they haven't come yet. We left our things at the stores till we could make up our minds which hotel —"

"Ten dollars," said the clerk, abruptly. Lorenzo

did not know why he said this, but he stood waiting behind the register, and it came to Lorenzo that he was asking ten dollars of him, and he took out his money and paid it rather tentatively. The clerk took the money, and said, as he laid it in a drawer, "We have to get it in advance where there's no baggage. Like to go to your room?"

"I guess we'll have some dinner first," said Lorenzo. He had decided that he would not try to answer yes or no to anything, for fear he should say yee or nay, and he found it easy to begin always with a guess.

"Early dinner from one to three," said the clerk. "Go in any time you like." He did not seem so unkind now as at first; he even smiled a little in looking at Lorenzo, as if now he had fathomed his hesitation in registering, and imagined him to have had the newly married man's embarrassment in declaring his condition so publicly for the first time. He even added, "Dining-room right through the parlor," and then he turned finally away.

Lorenzo went back to the place where he had left Althea. She was not there, and his heart gave a leap of alarm. He looked all round, whirling about, and searching the long verandas with eyes which he could not keep from being anxious.

Far off, almost at the end of the grove, two ladies — one in white and one in blue — were walking. At the moment he caught sight of them they stopped, and the one in blue began to wave her handkerchief as if she were signalling to him. Then he saw that it was Althea with that young woman who had taken his place beside her; it was she who was waving to him. She had Althea by the arm, and was leaning forward, as if talking rapidly up into her face. He went out to meet them, advancing shyly; and as soon as he came within hearing the young woman screamed at him, "Were you *scared*? Did you think some one had run away with her?"

Lorenzo was ashamed to own that he had been frightened. He said, "I guess so;" and that seemed to pass for a joke with the young woman, who bowed herself forward, and then threw herself backward in the fit of laughter that seized her at his words. She walked mincingly, and she hung her disengaged hand at her side with her handkerchief always in it, which she now pressed to her eyes, as if to wipe away her tears of laughter. She realized to Lorenzo all that he had ever dreamed of fashionable splendor in the world-outside. Her dress was beautiful, and so was her hat, which she wore at a saucy slant on her little golden head.

Althea blushed as they approached, but she merely said, "We thought you would see us; but we were coming back anyway."

"Oh, this is the best joke!" the young lady cried, beginning to laugh again. "I shall tell George about this the very first thing when I see him. I guess *he* wouldn't have been scared. He knows I couldn't be *induced* to run away from him. We did give you a scare, didn't we? Poor Mr. Brown!"

Lorenzo stared and said, "My name is Weaver."

"Why, your wife said it was Brown," the young lady began, in a tone of injury. Then she burst out laughing again. "Oh, I see!" She turned to Althea. "You forgot you were married, and you told me your maiden name. Oh, that is *too* good! When I tell George about this! But it isn't the least bit surprising. I've been married nearly a whole week, and I believe if I didn't keep saying my married name over to myself all the time, I shouldn't realize yet that I was married. But the only way is to keep saying it; and I write it too: Mrs. George Cargate, Mrs. George Cargate. If you don't do it, you'll get into all sorts of scrapes. Well, Mr. Weaver, I am going to be awfully good now, and leave you to yourselves; I can see that you're just dying to be together." She drew her arm out of Althea's, and then seized her by both wrists. "Oh, you are just too sweet for anything! That cherry red does become you so, and it's just the same shade here, and here, and here!" She touched the knot on Althea's hat, the knot on her breast, and the dimple on her check; and then, with a cry of laughter, she broke from them and ran down the path to the hotel.

Lorenzo and Althea stood abashed in each other's presence. "Well, well!" he said, at last.

"I presume we do not understand their ways yet," said Althea. "She seems to mean well; but she seems to let herself go a good deal, even for the world-outside."

"Oh yes," Lorenzo assented; "I presume she don't mean any harm by it. I'd rather see a person more settled."

They were walking demurely side by side towards the hotel, and she cast an upward, sidewise look at him. "You wouldn't like to have me start off now with a little scream and run after her, yonder?"

"Nay," said Lorenzo, soberly, "I should *not*, Althea." Something ascetic showed in his kind young face; the potentiality of Shaker eldership passed like a cloud-shadow over it. "I don't like such behaving. Did you tell her — did you make her understand — that we were not married yet?"

"Nay, there was no time for *that*," answered Althea; "I had to let her go on talking to me, as if we were."

"Yee," said Lorenzo.

"We had to let that driver think so too," she pursued.

"Oh yee," said Lorenzo, with a sigh; and he thought how he had let the hotel people think so by the entry he had made; but he did not tell Althea of that. "I presume," he said, with another deep breath, "that it is not deceiving unless we mean to deceive. It will be all right as soon as we *are* married."

"We promised not to talk of that yet," said Althea.

"Yee. Not till *you* say so. I guess it's about dinner-time now."

"Oh, well, then, let us go right in. I am hungry. It is a long time since we had breakfast."

# XI

AT the door of the dining-room, where Lorenzo gave his hat to a man who was taking hats and putting them on long shelves, they stopped.

"My short hair will show," Althea whispered, with her hands up to the elastic that held her hat on. "Shall you mind if it makes them look?"

"Oh nay, not if *you* don't," and he flushed a little, thinking how pretty she was, with her hands up so.

"I presume they will think it is queer. I don't know exactly what to do, Lorenzo."

They stood staring into the vast dining-room in a hesitation that grew painful. Rows of small tables stretched away in long perspective, with one wide avenue dividing them, and aisles penetrating their multitude crosswise and lengthwise. The china and glass and silver glittered, the napery shone, and the black waiters in white linen jackets ran to and fro seating and serving the guests, who were there already in great number. They kept pressing in around Lorenzo and

Althea where they stood. An old, gray-headed negro received them with severe state as they entered, and waved his hand to one of his subordinates, who beckoned to the guests and ran down the dining-hall before them to some table where he pulled out chairs for them to be seated.

"Well, well!" said Lorenzo, in vague response to Althea's perplexity; and he turned about without hope of help, but merely to gain time, when his eyes met the gay eyes of that young woman coming forward with her silent mother.

"Oh, are you going to have early dinner, too?" she called to him, and her voice made Althea turn round. "*We* are, just to pass away the time; we have got to do something till George comes. I've just got a despatch from him — he telegraphs twice a day — and only think! He won't be here till to-morrow morning. Isn't it a shame? I don't know what I'm going to do to live through it. Why don't you go in?" she asked Althea, as she put her hand through her arm. "We can go in together, I suppose; but there are no seats at our table, and they'll be sure to put you somewhere else, they're so obstinate. What are you waiting for?" She seemed to note something unusual now in their delay, and she addressed her question to Lorenzo.

"It's her short hair," he began; and in spite of Althea's "Oh, Lorenzo!" he went on, " It'll show so when she takes her hat off."

"Well, don't take it off, then!" cried the young woman. "Half of them are going in with their hats and bonnets on, don't you see?"

"Yee–es," said Lorenzo. "But we didn't know —"

"I guess you can do what other people do. Why did you cut it off? Was it sickness? I had a fever once when I was little, and I had to have my head *shaved*. George says he wishes he could have seen me." She was pressing into the room with her hand in Althea's arm, and the stately negro stopped them with a bow that made her drop her hand. "There! I suppose they'll put you off somewhere by yourselves. I think everything is too provoking to-day! But I'll see you just as soon as we're through dinner." She went gayly off with her mother, and an airy waiter went down, and in and out of the tables, in a series of dancing positions, till he had led Lorenzo and Althea almost the whole length of the hall, and pulled out two chairs for them where they were to sit, and snapped his fingers to another waiter, who came forward to wait upon them. They were red with shame and fear, but under his friendly smile they began to feel more at their ease. They did not know what to ask for, and they let him choose their dinner, which he brought in splendid profusion, and put before them with affectionate hospitality, which, after he had served their dessert, began to suffer a chill eclipse. He went and stood gloomily against the wall with folded arms.

"I can't think what it is comes over them all, Althea," said Lorenzo. "I believe I shall ask that young woman when we get back to the parlor and have a chance to speak to her."

He had not to wait so long. The young woman made her way to them from her distant table before they rose from theirs, and took a vacant seat beside Althea. When Lorenzo told how strangely the sleeping-car porter and the restaurant waiter and now this waiter had behaved towards the end, she laughed, and said, "Why, it must be the tip. Did you give them something."

"What for?"

"For waiting on you."

"I thought they were paid for that."

"Well, they are. But they always expect something extra, George says."

"Well, well!" said Lorenzo. "How much had I ought to give?"

"Well, George says — of course, I don't know anything about it myself — *George* says he always gives them five dollars to begin with, and that makes them pleasant; but if they don't look after him well after that he don't give them anything more."

Lorenzo took out his money, which he had all in one roll of bills, and peeled off a five-dollar note, which he held out towards the waiter. The waiter rushed upon it. When he recognized its value he burst into a joyous effervescence of thanks; he begged them to let him bring them something else, and overwhelmed them with finger-bowls and superfluous service; he went down on his knees under the table, to see if they had not dropped something; he said that he would be sure to keep those seats for them as long as they stayed; and he said he would speak to the head-waiter, so that they should not be shown elsewhere.

"Yes, I guess that was it," said the young woman, when they had got away from him, and were walking up the wide avenue towards the door together. She had her hand through Althea's arm again, and she talked to Lorenzo over her pretty shoulder, which she drew a little forward as she moved. "I guess you've fixed him. And now, Mr. Weaver, I'm going to ask a great favor of you. I want you to lend me your wife a little while. I want her to go shopping with me for an hour or so. I can't think of any other way to put in the time, and if I don't do something I shall simply go stark, staring, raving mad without George here. The stores in Saratoga are awfully nice, and I've seen a lot of things that I want to get, and I know Mrs. Weaver has seen things too that she wants."

"N–no," Althea began. "I have got everything. I don't want —"

"Now that is all nonsense," said the young woman. "You tell her it is, Mr. Weaver! I know she's dying to get something; and you give her a lot of money, won't you? It's your wedding journey, you know, and of course you expect to waste a little, and then economize after you settle down. That's what George says."

"Why, Althea, there may be something you need," Lorenzo suggested.

"Now I ain't going to have it that way!" the young woman pouted. "She's going to get what she *wants,* whether she *needs* it or not. That's the way I tell George I'm going to do, and I shall make the money fly, and he had better look out to get plenty of it. It drives mamma almost crazy to hear me talk, and she always takes his part against me."

"Do you want I should go, Lorenzo?" asked Althea; but there was a latent light in her eye, that pleaded when her words would not.

"Why, yee," said Lorenzo.

"Is that your pet way of saying yes?" asked the young woman. "I think it's awfully nice to have those pet words just between yourselves. George and I, we say *yep,* and *nop,* just for fun, you know, like children. Well, now, give her the money, Mr. Weaver, and we'll be back in the parlor about four o'clock, for I'm going to make an afternoon of it, and we're not going to have you round. You can go off and sit in the park — Congress Park, right over there — and listen to the music, or you can go off shopping for yourself if you want to. Mrs. Weaver, I want you to come up to my room while I get my walking-dress on, and I want you to see my trousseau. There's one imported dress — present from George — that is the *dreamiest* thing! By-by!" She waved her hand over her coquettishly shrugged shoulder, and without looking at Lorenzo again she pulled Althea away with her.

# XII

LORENZO sat in the park till he was tired; then he went about to the different shops where they had left things, and carried them to the hotel himself. He had to wait half an hour in the hotel parlor before Althea and the young woman came in. The young woman said she was dead tired, and she knew they were just dying to be together, and she ran off and left them.

"Lorenzo," said Althea, "can I go over and sit in that place where you have been staying? I want to talk with you. Can we talk there?"

"Why, yee. It's a very quiet place now; the people nearly all went away when the band stopped."

At the gate of the park Lorenzo stopped and bought admission tickets from the man at the window.

"Why, do you have to *pay* to go in?" demanded Althea.

"I found out I did when I tried to go in without," said Lorenzo. "You have to pay for pretty much everything in the world-outside."

"Oh, the world-outside, the world-outside!" cried the girl.

They walked along without speaking till they came to a seat where a recession in the high shaded bank made a special seclusion. They sat down, and Althea took from the belt of her dress a little roll of bank-notes and handed it to Lorenzo. "There is your money, Lorenzo — what is left of it. I spent some. I don't know how much. I am not used to counting it."

Lorenzo put the money in his pocket without looking at it. "Nay, we're neither of us much used to that, Althea. Did you get what you wanted?"

"I got what she said I ought to get; I got a travelling-dress! I told them to send the things to the hotel."

"Yee. And I went round to the places where we left our things this morning and got them."

"I had forgotten about those things," said Althea, dreamily. Lorenzo laughed vaguely, and she turned abruptly upon him, with a start from her absence. "Do you know what time it is, Lorenzo?"

"It *has* been rather of a long day, Althea, and I

guess you must have felt it so too. It seems to me, we've been about so, that it was back in the last century some time when we got out the cars this morning." He pulled his watch out, a large silver one, and he said, with an air of pride, as her eye fell upon it, "Friend Nason thought I better get it, seeing I never had one before, and he went with me to the jeweller's. It's a Swiss one, and it cost twelve dollars; he said it was full as good as an American one that would have cost me twenty." She seemed not to notice it, and he added, with a little disappointment, "It's half-past four." She did not say anything. He closed the case of his watch with a snap, and put it back in his pocket. "I was just thinkin'," he went on, in a smiling muse, "how this light lays along the slope of the upper pasture at the Family. Strikes over the top of the hill and slants along down; and it gets to be evening there, I guess, as much as an hour before it does in the lower pasture and the garden." He closed his eyes to a fine line. "I can see how it looks as plain as if I was there now. Rufus is comin' up the cow-path to look after the cows and drive 'em down to the barn; and I can see Elder Thomas there, waitin' with the boys to see 'em milk, and show 'em. It's just about the time your school lets out, and you're walkin' over to the Church Family house, and the children — Well, it's kind of peaceful there! And it's sightly. It's full as sightly here, I guess, and now the band's stopped it's peaceful too." The delicious breeze that had been freshening ever since morning was at its sweetest now; it sang through the tops of the tall, slim oaks of the park, and sighed in the clump of pines where they were sitting. Lorenzo paused, as if he hoped for some sympathetic response from Althea, and then he said, "But I like that upper pasture. I guess the thrushes are beginning to tune up about now in the wood-lot there. I sha'n't forget how you used to look comin' up by the walk, kind of bendin' forward, and lookin' for wild strawberries, with the little girls in the afternoons, a little later on —"

She broke in upon him with a sudden harshness: "Lorenzo, what was it made you feel foolish about me in the first place?"

Lorenzo kept the smile that was left from his muse, though Althea had spoken so strangely. "I don't know as I can remember the beginning exactly."

"Yee, you can, Lorenzo! There must have been a time when you began to feel foolish. Think!"

"Why, I told you, Althea. It was one day when I saw you in the march at meetin', and the way you stepped off, and the way you turned at the corners, and the way you carried your head. I always used to watch you; but that day I seemed to be following you round, as if I was drawed by a rope, and I couldn't get away if I tried."

"Was that what made you foolish about me?"

"It wasn't all. I don't know as I ought to tell you, Althea, but I thought you had beautiful eyes, and there was something about your mouth when you spoke or smiled, and your voice — there was something about that, when I picked it out in the singing; that seemed to go *through* me. I can't express it exactly."

"Was that all?"

"Well, I don't know as you want me to speak of it —"

"Yee, yee!" she besought him, passionately. "Tell me everything, speak of everything!"

"I thought — I thought you had a nice figure, Althea; I told you that last night. Your dress was the same as the rest, but it didn't look the same on you. It was sightlier, and graceful. There, I don't feel anyways sure it's right to speak of such things, but you wanted I should."

"Yee, I wanted you should. And now I am going to tell you what made me feel foolish about you. It was because you were so tall and strong-looking, and you had pretty eyelashes, and your hair had such a wave in it when it was long; and your mouth curved so at the corners, and you had such a deep voice. And you were so handsome; and once when we all went berrying, and I hurt my foot, and you lifted me over the wall —"

"I remember," said Lorenzo, joyfully, shyly.

"I didn't want you to put me down. Do you despise me for it?"

"Althea!"

"You were afraid I despised you for thinking I had a pretty figure." Lorenzo was silent, as if he did not know what to say.

"We've been over this before, Althea," he spoke, at last.

She did not heed what he said, apparently. "That young woman, that Mrs. Cargate, has been telling me all about her love affairs, as she calls them. She was engaged three times before she got married. She says she has been in love with lots of men."

"Well, well!" said Lorenzo.

"And she has got their pictures, and they have got hers. She asked me if I had been engaged before. She says it's nothing to be engaged. She says that her husband says he first felt foolish about her when he saw her through the car-window eating candy and carrying on, as she calls it, with some other girls; and it was her regular teeth, and red lips when she was eating, that made him feel so."

"It's kind of — sickish," said Lorenzo.

"He came into the car, and he made an excuse to sit down by her when the other girls left, and she let him have a chance to squeeze her hand — he didn't know that she let him —"

"Don't, Althea!"

"And before she got out they were as good as engaged; she was dead in love with him, she says, from the first look, and he sent her his picture as soon as he got to New York."

"Well, well!"

"Her mother was opposed to her getting engaged again because she thought it was just another flirtation, and she had got sick of having her engaged so much. She told me just why she fell in love with each one, and what each one said he fell in love with her for."

"It don't seem exactly right," said Lorenzo. "She must have made you about sick with her talk."

"Her mother didn't like him when he first called — they promised to correspond before she got off the cars, and she told him where she lived — but she took to her bed, and her mother had to consent. Now her mother likes him as much as she does. They're the greatest friends, and when he found that he would have to go back to New York from here he kept it a secret from her and telegraphed for her mother to come up and stay with her, and she never knew anything about it till her mother came into the room."

"Well, it seems to have come all right, then," said Lorenzo, with a vague optimism but he moved uneasily under Althea's eye, and his smile faded.

"From all that I can make out," she said, "they fell in love with each other for the same things, or just about the same, as we got foolish about each other for. He thought she was handsome, and she thought he was handsome. Lorenzo, they fell in love with each other's *looks!*"

Lorenzo waited a moment before he said, with a certain reproach, "I thought you was smart too, Althea — smarter than I was."

"And I knew you were good, Lorenzo. But it didn't begin with that."

"Nay, it didn't begin with that," he owned.

"If it had begun with that," she went on, "I shouldn't ever have doubted about it for a second. It's the way it began that makes me afraid of it."

"I never saw it in that light before," said Lorenzo.

She drew a little away from him, and looked at him askance. "How do I know but I was trying to make you feel, all the time in the march, that I was graceful? How do I know but what I just thought my foot hurt, so that you would *have* to carry me —"

"Now, look here, Althea, that young woman has made you blame yourself for nothin'. You're perfectly notionate about it —"

She caught his hand where it lay next her on

the seat, and pressed it nervously, piteously. "*Try to think back* — far back, Lorenzo — and see if there was not something different in your mind that made you foolish about me before you noticed that I was — sightly. See if you didn't think I was bright *first*. I shouldn't want them to say in the Family that we were taken with each other's *looks.*"

Lorenzo thought, as he was bid. "Nay, I guess it was the looks first, as far as *I* went," he said, faithfully. "It was afterwards that I thought you was smart."

"Oh!" she said, and a little gush of tears came into her eyes.

They were both silent for a time, and then Lorenzo said, "I know it seems kind of demeanin', but I don't know as you can say it's wrong exactly. I presume it's the way that folks have begun to feel foolish ever since — there was any folks. And I presume the looks must have been given to us for some good purpose?" He suggested rather than asserted this, with his eyes fastened tenderly upon Althea's face, which, blurred with tears as it was, was still so pretty. She wiped her eyes with the handkerchief he

126

had bought her that morning, and then tucked it, with a little vivid, graceful motion, into the waist of her dress.

When he began again it was with more confidence, more authority of tone. "The way I think we had ought to look at it is this: It's the body that contains the soul, and the body is outside of the soul, and it comes first, and it has a right to, as long as it's outside the soul. It can't help it, and the soul can't help it. But I believe we shall find each other in the soul more and more."

"Do you really think that, Lorenzo?"

"Yee, I do, and I wouldn't say it just to comfort you."

"I know you wouldn't, Lorenzo. You are true — truer than I am."

She rose, and they walked silently out of the park together. Beyond the gate he asked her, "Where would you like to go now, Althea?"

"To the minister's," she said.

Lorenzo arrested her in a panic. "Not unless you want to go there of your own accord, Althea."

"I do."

"Do you feel as if I had coaxed you to do it —

hurried you any?"

"Nay, you always do what you say you will do. If I only felt as sure of myself as I do of you!"

"Oh, I do!" said Lorenzo. "I presume," he continued, as if from the necessity of finding a reason for her conclusion, "you'll feel full better about lettin' that driver and the young woman think we're married if we really *are* married."

"Nay, what difference does that make now?" she demanded, scornfully.

"I don't know as it does a great deal," he assented.

"If we're like the world-outside in one thing, we must be like it in all," she said.

Lorenzo did not answer.

# XIII

IT was the minister himself again who opened the lattice door to them. "Oh, here you are back. I am glad to see you. Well, have you made up your minds?" He spoke while they were getting through the entry into his dim parlor, with a tone of pleasantry.

Althea took the word. "Yee, we have made up our minds."

"And you really intend to get married this time?" He looked at Lorenzo.

"Yee, we do."

"I suppose you've thought it over thoroughly. I wish all the young people who come to me would do so. It would save a great deal of hopeless and useless thinking afterwards. If you'll sit down I will call my wife, and —"

He left them alone a moment, and Lorenzo whispered, "Althea, if you want to ask him again how he looks at that point in Luke —"

"Nay, we can see it as clearly as he can. We have got all the light there is."

"Yee, I presume that is so."

They had each other by the hand, and she pressed his hand convulsively, "Don't say anything more, Lorenzo."

"Just as you say, Althea."

After a little delay the minister returned, bringing his wife with him — a short, stout little brunette, who had the effect of having hurriedly encased herself for the occasion in a black silk dress she wore. She glanced at Althea with a certain dislike or defiance in her look, as one does at a stranger whom one has heard prejudicial things of; and if the minister had told her of Althea's misgivings it might well have incensed a wife and mother.

He introduced them to her as Miss Brown and Mr. Weaver, and he said, "Well, now, if you will take your places," and when they stood before him he began the ceremony.

Lorenzo, when he was asked if he would take Althea to be his wedded wife, helplessly answered, "Yee," and Althea did the same in her turn.

The light of a smile came over the minister's face at their answers, and when he had pronounced them man and wife and blessed them, he said, laughing, "I suppose that this comes as near being a Shaker wedding as any could. Did you make the responses purposely in Shaker parlance?"

"Did we say yee?" Lorenzo asked of Althea.

"Yee, we did," she said, and he smiled, but she did not. "I heard *you* say it, and I guess I did."

They both sat down again, and the minister's wife was about to sit down too, seeing that they were not going away, when there came loud cries of grief and rage from the back of the house, and she ran out to still them. The minister went to a writing-desk and filled up a certificate of marriage, which he handed to Althea, and then he sat down too.

"I don't know why we always make the ladies the custodians of these things, but we do. I think myself it's often quite as important to the husband to know that he is married.

"And are we married now?" she faltered. "Is that all?"

"Quite. It wasn't so very formidable, was it?"

"But — but —" She stopped, as if in a fright. "But it isn't *over*? I thought — I thought there was something more; and that — that — Do you mean that now we couldn't change?"

"Why, surely," said the minister, "you understood what you were doing? Didn't you suppose that when I asked you if you would take this man for your husband, I was asking you if you would marry him?"

"Yee, I knew that. But I didn't think that was all there was to it."

"I presume," Lorenzo began, "that it's because you ain't used to it, Althea."

The minister broke in with a laugh. "It's to be hoped that you won't get into the habit of it, Mrs. Weaver; some people do. But you're quite right about it, in one sense. This isn't all there is of marriage, and it isn't all over by any means. It's just begun." He sat rocking and smiling at them, and they remained rigidly upright in their chairs.

"I presume," said Lorenzo, "that there's some charge. How much will it be?"

The minister seemed amused at the bluntness of the demand. "There's no fee." He had apparently a little difficulty in adding, "It is something we always leave to the bridegroom."

Lorenzo took out his roll of bank-notes. He peeled one off the roll, and handed it to the minister. "That be enough?"

The minister took the ten-dollar note and looked at it. "I think it would be altogether too much unless you are richer than I imagine."

"Well," said Lorenzo, proudly, "I started with a hundred dollars last night."

"And is that all your worldly wealth?"

"I've got a lot in Fitchburg that's worth four hundred more."

"Is that so?" asked the minister. "You are a capitalist. Still, I think that if you happen to have a one-dollar bill in that roll I should prefer it."

"I guess I got one," said Lorenzo, with the same phlegm; and he looked among the notes till he found a dollar bill, which he gave to the minister.

"Ah, thank you," said the minister; and he added, "I don't suppose you had quite the training of a financier — a moneyed man — in the Family?"

Lorenzo laughed. "I never had a cent in my hands till a week ago, when I left the Family. The Trustees do all the buyin'."

"Is it possible, is it possible?" cried the minister. "You are of the resurrection, indeed! You begin to convert me! Do you think they would admit me to the Family?"

"Oh, yee," said Lorenzo, gravely. "You would have to separate, and give up your children."

"Ah, that isn't so simple. At any rate, it requires reflection. But to be in a condition where the curse of money is taken away! What is the name of your family: Eden? Paradise? Golden Age?"

"Nay," returned Lorenzo, with seriousness; "we came from Harshire."

There seemed to be nothing more to say or do, but Lorenzo would probably not have got away of his own motion. It was Althea who had to say to the minister, "Well, good-afternoon;" and when he offered his hand in response, it was she who had first to take it. She did it very stiffly, but Lorenzo gave it a large, loose grasp, and held it a moment, as if trying to think of something grateful, or at least fitting, before he said, "Well, good-afternoon," in his turn.

# XIV

ON their way back to the hotel they were silent till Lorenzo took out the money he had put loosely into his pocket, and folded it more neatly. He turned the notes over, and then felt in his other pockets, as if he thought he might have misplaced some of them. Althea did not seem to notice what he was doing. She walked rapidly a little ahead of him.

"Althea," he said, gently, and a little timidly, "I don't know as we better stay in Saratoga — well, not a great deal longer." She looked round. "I — I — the money seems to be nearly all gone. I guess we ha'n't got much more than enough to pay for our tickets back to Fitchburg."

She appeared not to understand at first. Then she said, passionately, "Let us go at once then! I shall be glad to go. Don't let's stay a minute longer. It's *dreadful* to me here!"

"Just as you say, Althea," he returned, submissively. "I presume we might full as well stay till

after supper. We've paid for it, and the cars
don't —"

"Go and see if there isn't an earlier train — if
there isn't one that starts right off. I want to start
*now.*"

"Why, Althea —"

"Don't try to speak to me, Lorenzo!"

"Nay, I won't, then. But I got to take you to
the hotel, and get them to show you where the
room is."

"Well!"

"And then I'll go round to the depot and find
out about the cars."

As they mounted the steps of the hotel porch
a girlish figure in light blue came flying towards
them from the end of the long veranda. It was
young Mrs. Cargate; she waved a telegram in the
air. "Oh, he's coming!" she called to them. "He's
coming to-night! He'll be here on the seven
o'clock train! Oh, it seems as if I could *fly,* I'm so
glad! I could just hug everybody! I must hug
somebody; I must kiss —" She ran upon Althea,
and flung her arms round her, and put up her
pouted lips.

Althea pulled away, and, with her head

thrown back, "Nay," she said, icily, "we don't kiss."

The young woman released her. "You don't *kiss*? Well, if that isn't the best joke yet! When I tell George about this! Why, what do you and Mr. Wea —"

"It's against our religion," said Lorenzo, sternly, and his face was the face of an ascetic as he spoke.

The young woman gasped, and retreated from them, staring at them as she paced slowly backward. She turned and ran, with a cry of laughter, towards the black figure of her silent mother at the end of the veranda.

At the door of their room Lorenzo left Althea. "I will go and see about the cars now. You get the things all ready, so that we needn't lose any time if the cars start anyways soon." He spoke with an austerity which was like something left of the tone he had used in rebuking that young woman. It was gone when he came back, and called gently, on the outside of the door, "Althea!"

"Yee, Lorenzo," her voice answered, "come in!"

He opened the door, and stood staring at her

from the threshold. She sat dressed in her garb of Shakeress — the plain, straight gown of drab, the drab shawl crossed upon her breast, the close collar that came up to her chin; her face was hidden in the depths of the Shaker bonnet.

"Well, well!" he murmured, huskily.

"Sit down, Lorenzo," she said.

"There ain't much time, Althea. The cars start in about half an hour, and —" he glanced about the room, where, on chairs and sofas, were strewn the finery that Althea had worn during the day; the packages of her afternoon purchases had been torn open, and their contents scattered about on the floor. His eye caught upon a fashionable gown of gray stuff. "That your travelling-dress, Althea?" he asked, feebly.

"I have got on my travelling-dress, Lorenzo. I am going back to the Family."

"Yee," he vaguely assented.

"I tried to put that dress on," she continued; "I couldn't." She paused, as if for him to say something, but he did not say anything. "I have thought it all out at last, Lorenzo. I don't blame the earthly order; it's the best thing there is in the world-outside. But we have known the heavenly order, and if — even if — we were to be very happy together —"

She stopped, and he said," Yee."

"Or, that isn't it, either. They may be all wrong in what they taught us in the Family."

Lorenzo cleared his throat. "It did seem so — for a spell."

"But whether it was right or whether it was wrong, whether it was true or whether it was false, *it's too strong for me now,* and it would be too strong as long as I lived. I have got to go back."

"Have you thought what they will say?"

"Haven't I thought what they would say every minute since I stole out of the Family house like a thief and ran away? But I don't care what they will say. They will take me back, I know that, and that is all I care for."

"Yee."

"I want you should let me go as far as Fitchburg with you, and then I can easily get to Harshire."

He stared at her. "Althea, do you think I am going to let you go back *alone?*" he asked, solemnly. "I am going back to Harshire with you."

"Nay, Lorenzo, I have thought that out too. I

blame myself for getting married to you."

"I wanted to full as much as you did, Althea. It was my fault too."

"I thought — I thought if it was over I should feel differently, and see it as folks do in the world-outside."

"Yea, I knew that, Althea. I wouldn't have let you if I hadn't understood it so. I could see how your mind was workin'."

"But I can't see it so, Lorenzo! The more I look at it the worse it seems for us!"

"It's strange," he mused, aloud, "that we can't look at it in their light. Is it a sin for all the world?"

"It isn't a sin for the world, for the world hasn't the same light as ours. But we should be shutting our eyes to the light!"

"Yee," he assented, sadly.

"But, Lorenzo," she entreated, passionately, "if you *say* for me to stay in the world-outside with you and be your wife, I will do it! Do you say so? Do you say so?" She came towards him with her hands clasped, and her face wild in the depths of her Shaker bonnet, where her tears shone dimly. "I'm nothing! What do I care for myself?

140

It's only the truth I care for, and the light! But if you say so, Lorenzo, the light of the world shall be *my* light, the *darkness* shall be my light!"

There was a moment before he answered, "Nay, I don't say so, Althea!"

"Oh!" She fell back in her chair and began to sob.

"Do you think," he asked, "that I could be anyways comfortable knowin' that you wanted to live the angelic life, and I was draggin' you down to the earthly?"

"The angelic life wouldn't be anything without you, Lorenzo," she said, tenderly, but with a confusion of purpose which was not, perhaps, apparent even to herself.

"Nor the earthly order without you," he answered, solemnly. He added, with that mixture of commonplace which was an element in his nature, "I presume, if I wanted to stay in the world-outside, I could get a divorce easy enough; but if I can't have you, I don't want to stay. If you can't feel that it's right for you to live in the earthly order, I know it can't be right for me either. We can do like so many of them have done: we can go back to the Family, and live there separate. It will be a cross, but it won't be any more of a cross for us than it is for the others that have separated; and maybe — maybe we ought to bear a cross."

"Don't *try* to make me cry, Lorenzo!"

He looked round the room again, disordered with the pretty things she had flung about. "I declare," he said, dreamily, "that hat's got to look like you."

"Lorenzo!"

"If you've got on everything you need, Althea, we'll leave these things here. We sha'n't want 'em any more where we're goin'." He stopped, and they stood looking at each other. "Althea, we have got to tell them everything we've done when we get back."

"Yee."

"Do you believe, Althea," he said, in a voice that came like a thick whisper from his throat, "that they would think any the worse of you if I was to — kiss you?"

"I don't know, Lorenzo."

"It would be for good-bye, just once; and it would be my fault, and not yours."

"I don't want you should bear the blame. If

you were to do it, it would be — because I let you."

He caught her to his breast; she laid her arms tenderly about his neck; their heads were both hidden in her Shaker bonnet.

"Now come," he said.

They walked along towards the station rapidly, Lorenzo some paces ahead of Althea, and they looked as if they did not belong together. A young fellow in a light wood-colored surrey, with a pair of slender sorrels, drew up to the sidewalk, and called to Lorenzo, "Carriage! Want a ca—" His eye strayed from Lorenzo to the figure of Althea in her Shaker dress. He pushed up his hat, and the cigar which he was smoking dropped from his parting lips. They passed him without looking up, but his head was drawn round after them, as if by a magnetic attraction, and he remained staring at them over his shoulder till they were lost to sight at the corner turning to the station.

THE END

# GREEN INTEGER
Pataphysics and Pedantry

Douglas Messerli, *Publisher*

Essays, Manifestos, Statements, Speeches, Maxims,
Epistles, Diaristic Notes, Narratives, Natural Histories,
Poems, Plays, Performances, Ramblings, Revelations
and all such ephemera as may appear necessary
to bring society into a slight tremolo of confusion
and fright at least.

\*

## MASTERWORKS OF FICTION

Masterworks of Fiction is a program of Green Integer
to reprint important works of fiction from all centuries.
We make no claim to any superiority of these fictions
over others in either form or subject, but rather we
contend that these works are highly enjoyable to read
and, more importantly, have challenged the ideas and
language of the times in which they were published,
establishing themselves over the years as among
the outstanding works of their period. By republishing
both well known and lesser recognized titles in this series
we hope to continue our mission bringing our society
into a slight tremolo of confusion and fright at least.